SMALL GREAT JOYS

RESILIENT HEARTS HISTORICAL ROMANCE SERIES BOOK 1

DANIELLE CARRIERE

Copyright © 2021 by Danielle Carriere

Originally published in 2019 as *Angel*

Cover design by Lynn Andreozzi

ISBN 978-1-7329095-8-8 (paperback)

ISBN 978-1-7329095-7-1 (ebook)

Published by Moxie Books

www.authordaniellecarriere.com

To Mom and Dad, for giving me courage.

AUTHOR'S NOTE

My books do not have particularly graphic content. However, I recognize that everyone has different lived experiences and preferences, and I want to be respectful of that. Notes on content can be found on my website underneath the details for each book:

www.authordaniellecarriere.com

1

I saved my brother's life once. Every day since then, I've wished I let him die. Does that make me more like Cain or Abel, I wonder?

∼

NEBRASKA, 1880

Nathan crossed his arms, leaned back against the wooden post behind him, and surveyed the dust-choked street with guarded eyes. The buildings of the small town blocked any breath of wind that might have ventured to pass through, and the air felt stagnate and dirty. Nathan cast a glance over his shoulder at the pristine white front of the general store. It looked newly painted, but no amount of fresh paint would ever cover up the distaste Nathan felt for this place.

The saloon across the street was lifeless. It had been lifeless when Nathan arrived in town to submit his claim for a land deed, and now, less than a day later, its state had not improved. Nathan suspected the saloon had not been frequented by patrons for some time. It was funny how a building so empty could hold so many memories.

For several long moments, Nathan warred with himself. It had been seven years since he had last passed through Oklada. Seven years since he had spent an afternoon outside the saloon while his father drank inside. Seven years since he had met Angel.

She had been a child then, only a few years younger than Nathan himself. In the years since, Nathan had sworn he would never return to Oklada, and it was only out of necessity that Nathan found himself here once again. Even so, he couldn't deny the pull the empty saloon had held over him since he had arrived.

Nathan turned and walked into the general store, removing his hat as he entered. He needed answers.

The owner of the store smiled as Nathan approached the counter, hat in hand. "What can I help you to find?"

Nathan shook his head. "I'm afraid I'm only looking for information today."

The owner continued smiling. "Well, time is money, but talk is cheap, and information is free. What can I help you with?"

Nathan took a deep breath, then said, "I'd like to know how long the saloon has been closed."

The owner's eyes narrowed, growing calculating, but his smile remained. The combination gave him a hungry, wolfish look. "It's been closed for a couple months now. The owner was shot. Some sort of disagreement that got out of hand."

Nathan considered the man's words for a moment before asking, "There was a girl. Angel?"

The storekeeper gave him a look so filthy it made Nathan want to wash his hands clean of the question he had asked.

"Son, just how well did you know her—Angel?" The shopkeeper chose his words carefully, deliberately.

Nathan replied in like measure. "I only ever knew her name and part of her story."

The shopkeeper relaxed, then leaned forward, speaking in a conspiratorial tone. "Well then, I'll tell you, man to man, there's at least one man who knew her better than you, if you take my meaning."

Nathan understood. "Man to man"—his words were curt— "should I take your meaning to understand you knew her well?"

The storekeeper's eyes widened under his rising eyebrows, and his words nearly tripped over themselves in his hurried denial. "Oh, good heavens, no." He cast furtive glances around himself, then stated emphatically, "My wife and I are very happily married. Very happily."

Nathan nodded absently, then asked, "Where is she now?"

"My wife?" asked the storekeeper in surprise. At Nathan's withering glance, the man gave a forced laugh, then said, "Oh yes, of course, the girl."

The storekeeper paused, then shrugged. "I don't rightly know." He scrubbed thoughtfully at his beard. "She came in here two, maybe three days ago. Wanted to buy some supplies. Looked like she might be readying herself to move on and find a new place to settle. No one's seen her since."

Nathan waited for the storekeeper to continue, but when the man said nothing more, Nathan said, "I'm much obliged for the information. I'll be on my way now."

Snapping out of his daze, the storekeeper spoke sympathetically. "Son, I think I know how you feel, but you're better off without her. Those females—they're silly, unreliable things."

Already halfway through the door, Nathan paused, then bit his tongue and kept walking. No matter. The saloon was closed, Angel was gone, Nathan had gotten the land deed he had come for, and one way or the other, he would not be coming back to this place.

Nathan climbed into the wagon, then clucked his tongue and lifted the reins of the team in front of him. The wagon creaked forward with a jolting motion. The team of horses quickly found their natural rhythm, and Nathan found himself settling into the familiar rock and sway of the wagon. He relaxed his hold on the leather reins and leaned back, resting a foot on the board in front of him. The horses knew their way home and were eager be there—they needed little guidance on the return trip.

The sun filtered down through the green leaves above, casting dancing shadows on the earth of the road. The sunlight still carried the familiar sweetness of summer smells and warmth, but the shadows underneath held an almost imperceptible chill, a reminder of the approaching fall.

Unlike past years, the whisper of colder weather did not fill Nathan with apprehension. It had been a good year and a productive warm season. He had chinked the cracks in the walls of his cabin and patched a hole in the roof of the barn. Both would be warm and cozy when the snow and cold winds came. He had plenty of firewood and feed for the animals. He had wheat to make flour, a root cellar stocked full of potatoes and carrots, apples and onions, beets and squash, and plenty of smoked venison to last through the winter season. He was confident that, for the first time he could remember in all of his nineteen years, it would be a comfortable winter. It was amazing how far money could go when it wasn't being squandered on liquor.

As the wagon rounded the first curve in the road and the town—now only a speck on the horizon—fell out of view behind Nathan, a female figure appeared on the road ahead, walking with her back toward him.

Angel. Even though Nathan knew the girl on the road couldn't be Angel—if what the storekeeper had said was true, Angel would be miles away by now—the thought came to his mind unbidden. He immediately forced it away, but it lodged stubbornly in his chest.

Angel.

Nathan had missed her by three days, maybe less, but he had no way of knowing where she was going or how far she could have traveled in three days' time. Maybe if distance had been the only obstacle, Nathan would have allowed himself to wonder whether he might still be able to find her. But now, even though there were fewer miles between them than there had been in years, as far as Nathan was concerned, he and Angel were just as far apart as they had always been.

Nathan clenched his jaw and let out a disgusted breath, fighting to hear against the dull roar that had filled his ears ever since the shopkeeper in the town had spoken the words, "I'll tell you, man to man . . ."

The words rubbed raw like a burr under a horse's saddle blanket. Nathan didn't know what else he had expected. Angel had been a child when he had met her seven years ago, but she would have since grown up. And with her uncle owning the saloon, well, it shouldn't have been surprising that she would have followed in his footsteps.

Nathan shook his head. Nearly at the same time, the mare on the left shook her head as though she were ridding herself of a pesky fly, causing the buckles on the harness to jangle and Nathan to realize that in his frustration he had been unintentionally pulling back on the reins. He forced himself to relax, and the horses again settled into a steady rhythm.

The distance between the wagon and the girl slowly closed until they were nearly side by side. Nathan wouldn't have given the girl a second glance, but as he drew up behind her, she stepped off to the side of the road to let him pass. She raised a hand to shield her eyes as she watched him, and the movement drew his attention. He knew he should offer her a ride, but he guiltily tried to ignore the thought —the last thing he wanted was to stop and talk to anyone—but once the thought entered his mind, it refused to be pushed out.

Nathan sighed and rubbed his knuckles against the bridge between his eyes, then pulled back on the reins and spoke to stop the horses. They shuffled their feet impatiently, causing the metal buckles in the harness to jangle, but they stood in place. The girl faced him as the wagon halted next to her, her bonnet keeping Nathan from seeing her face in its entirety.

Nathan spoke without enthusiasm, hoping the girl would decline his offer. "Can I give you a ride somewhere, Miss?"

"That depends a great deal on where you are going."

The young woman's tone was polite but cool, and Nathan cringed internally, knowing that in his voice she had heard the irritation he felt. Nathan nodded in the direction his team was facing, then spoke, trying to force some note of warmth into his voice. "Right now, it looks like the same way you are."

The girl paused for a moment, her gaze following the empty dirt road stretching out in front of them. Nathan suspected she knew there were a good few miles from where they stood to the next town. As reluctant as she might be to accept his offer of help, he knew she would—there was neither a graceful exit to the situation nor a reason to create one.

She nodded slightly. "Much obliged."

Nathan reached a hand down to help the girl into the wagon. She accepted his offer, lightly placing her hand in his and raising a foot to rest on one of the spokes of the front wheel. Nathan's muscles tensed as he braced himself to lift her into the wagon, and the girl looked up, preparing to step away from the ground. As she did so, the sun caught her face beneath the shadow of her bonnet. A jolt of recognition flashed through Nathan, and a memory he had tried to push into the back corners of his mind, one that had simultaneously tormented and sustained him over the past seven years, rushed forward to claim its place.

"ANGEL?" twelve-year-old Nathan scoffed. "Is that your real name?"

All wide, brown eyes, the girl Angel met his gaze with earnest curiosity. "It is. Don't you like it?"

In that moment, something shifted inside of Nathan, and he wanted nothing more than to protect that wide-eyed innocence. His voice softened. "Nah, it's a fine name."

Nathan's words were rewarded with a slight smile. Then, her expression suddenly growing intent, Angel said, "Horsefly. Don't move," and with a familiarity that didn't seem to cause her a moment's pause, she slapped Nathan's back.

"Got him," Angel said with satisfaction.

Her gesture took Nathan by surprise, and he was unprepared for the pain that lanced through his body at her touch. Nathan flinched, then caught himself, glancing around to see who might be watching.

Angel jerked her hand away. "What's wrong? What did I do? I'm sorry, I didn't know—" The apologies spilled rapidly from Angel's lips until Nathan smiled faintly and waved a dismissive hand. He knew his smile didn't move past the stiff muscles of his cheeks—his teeth were still gritted from the shock of pain—but it was the best he could manage.

"It's nothing. My back's just tore up some."

His attempt to dismiss Angel's concern was in vain, and the furrow between her brows deepened. "Let me see."

Nathan shook his head. "It's nothing."

But the concern on Angel's face remained, an insistent question lingering in her eyes, and Nathan knew she would persist either until Nathan left or until he told her what she wanted to know.

Nathan closed his eyes and let out a long breath of air. Even if he would have had somewhere else to go, he was too tired to do so. As he saw it, that left him with three options. He could tell her a lie she wouldn't believe. He could tell her the truth and leave no doubt. Or, he could show her the truth and let her draw her own conclusions.

Nathan opened his eyes to again meet Angel's curious stare. Glancing around to make sure no one was near, he reached around to raise the back of his shirt just high enough for her to see skin laced with lacerations and darkened with deep, ugly bruises in various stages of healing. Angel exhaled softly, and at that small noise, Nathan jerked his shirt back down.

"It's nothing. It'll heal."

Nathan wanted to be able to laugh, to explain and shrug her worries away, and to tell her a story about falling out of trees, or off horses or barns, or anything but the truth. But it was too late. Angel turned her eyes toward the doors of the saloon they sat in front of, and Nathan knew she had already seen more than he'd intended to show. When she turned back to meet his gaze, Nathan looked away, giving a tight nod to confirm what Angel already knew. His father.

Angel paused and then, raising a finger indicating for him to wait, rose and walked back inside. She returned with a small jar. "Turn around," she commanded.

"What is that?" he asked.

Angel raised an eyebrow and, placing one hand on her hip, motioned with the other hand—still holding the mysterious jar—for him to turn. She looked uncannily matronly for someone so young. Nathan hesitated, then turned so that his back was toward her, and slowly pulled up his shirt again. He braced himself for the sting of alcohol, but as she began to smooth the salve on his wounded back, he felt only the unfamiliar sensation of pain leaving his body. His shoulders untensed, and he began to breathe again— he hadn't even realized he had stopped.

When she finished, he slowly pulled his shirt back down. He had expected the feeling of coarse fibers catching on raw skin, but instead, the salve created a slight, soft barrier. To his torn back, it felt like heaven.

The thought left his lips almost as soon as it entered into his head. "You really are an angel."

2

A few years later, my brother saved my life. Maybe he thought that made us even, but saving my life was no favor. I would have been better off if he would have let me die that day—I ran out of reasons to live a long time ago.

THE MEMORY SEEMED to last for ages. In reality, it had lasted only a few seconds. Angel's eyes widened in shock as she recognized Nathan, and forgetting that her foot rested on the wheel of the wagon and not the ground, she pulled her hand from his and tried to step back, stumbling and nearly losing her balance. Nathan guessed that with the sun behind him, Angel had not recognized him until she had reached out to take his hand and stepped into his shadow—the same moment he had recognized her.

"What are you doing here?" Nathan's voice rasped as the question passed his lips. He remembered asking a similar question years ago, but this time, his words were sharp, not sad.

Angel's initial smile of recognition disappeared, then faded into a distance that Nathan knew mirrored his own. Her eyes hardened, creating a countenance so different from the wide-eyed openness he remembered that Nathan caught himself glaring back at her. He tried to relax the creases around his eyes, but only succeeded in uncomfortably raising both eyebrows.

Angel folded her arms across her chest and stepped backward as she answered his question. "Leaving."

"Where are you going?"

Angel gave him a long, appraising look. When she spoke, it wasn't in answer to his question. "I should be on my way. I have a long ways to go."

"A long ways to go where?" Nathan pressed.

Angel looked down the road, the same direction she had been walking and that Nathan had been traveling, but her gaze focused far beyond any distant horizon either she or Nathan could have seen. She shook her head, then said simply, "Away."

Nathan felt a flash of irritation, but a quick glance told him that Angel wasn't trying to be evasive. There was no defiance in her eyes. Away was the truth as far as she knew it.

Nathan closed his eyes and exhaled loudly. "Do you still want a ride?" he asked curtly. As little as he wanted this conversation to continue, he couldn't quite bring himself to drive away and leave her standing on the side of the road. Unless, as he hoped, Angel requested that he do exactly that.

Nathan watched Angel's pride war with exhaustion. Practicality won out as she shifted her weight and winced, favoring one of her ankles. "Yes," she said stiffly, "I would be grateful for the ride."

Inwardly, Nathan groaned, but he offered her his hand again and, after slight hesitation, Angel took it and climbed onto the wagon and into the seat next to him. He lifted the reins, and the horses began their homeward journey once more.

THEY SAT IN SILENCE, *side by side, on the dusty wooden stairs in front of the*

saloon. Nathan was glad for Angel's quiet companionship, but he couldn't help feeling anxious as they waited.

Finally, in an attempt to stave off the self-reflection that silence always brought, he spoke. "How old are you, anyway?" he asked.

"Ten. You?"

"Twelve."

"What are you doing here?"

She shrugged. "It's a long story."

"I've probably got a long time." He jerked his head toward the saloon doors in explanation.

"It's not a very happy story." Angel watched Nathan's face as she spoke, gauging his reaction to her words.

He spoke, not dismissively, but matter-of-factly. "Neither is mine."

She nodded slightly, then turned her gaze to focus on the lines she had been drawing in the dirt with the toe of her boot, not meeting his eyes as she spoke.

"About a year ago, I was traveling with my parents. We were on a steamboat. One of the engines exploded and started a fire. Most of the passengers got off in time, but my mother and father were both killed. Tom —the man who runs the saloon here—was my father's brother and my nearest next of kin, so they sent me here to live with him."

Angel paused, then shrugged as she saw Nathan's expectant expression. "That's about all of it."

Nathan thought there was probably a great deal more to it than she had told him. He cast a contemptuous glance toward the saloon behind him and asked, "And how does he—Tom—treat you?"

Angel shrugged again, but her eyes were sad. "He treats me fine. I miss my parents. It's different here. My father was a doctor. Tom doesn't really know what to do with a ten-year-old girl."

Raising an eyebrow, Nathan shot a sideways glance at Angel. She sounded confident as she spoke, but her last words sounded more someone else's than her own. Nathan phrased his next question carefully. "And what do you do here now?"

"Keep the saloon clean, mostly. Sometimes I have to help the ladies here." Angel lowered her voice then continued. "Sometimes some of the men *who come are mean to the ladies. They hurt them. Tom never lets those men come back."*

Nathan felt cold, even though it was the middle of summer. He ran his hand through his hair, exhaling in disgust and speaking under his breath. "I bet."

He met her eyes, expecting to see understanding, but all he saw was sad, dark-eyed innocence.

Just then, the silence was broken by the sound of boots on wood, and three men pushed their way through the swinging doors of the saloon. One of the men, flanked on either side by the remaining two, was obviously being forcibly shown out. Nathan ducked his head as shame colored his neck a deep red. It was his father.

Nathan's father stood dazed for a moment. He looked blearily around, and then his eyes seemed to focus and latch on to Nathan. Nathan's father strode purposefully, if not steadily, forward, then grabbed his son's arm and dragged him to his feet without slowing down. "Let's go, Nathan. We're not welcome here."

As Nathan was pulled upwards, one of the men spoke. "Angel, your uncle needs you inside."

Angel rose to her feet, and with a backward glance, disappeared through the swinging doors of the saloon. Nathan, following behind his father, hung his head and wished he could disappear.

3

My brother gave me my life, but he destroyed everything in it that mattered—my father, my reputation, my girl—and left nothing but pieces shattered so sharply that to touch them was to bleed.

ANGEL AND NATHAN traveled without conversation. Nathan was grateful for the sounds of the creaking wagon, and the rocks rolling beneath the wheels, and the chirping birds. They filled what otherwise would have been a silent void, easing some of the tension he felt.

"How far until you leave the main road?" Angel broke the not-quite silence.

"About a mile on the other side of town, so I'll be able to drop you off as we pass through." Nathan glanced sideways at her as he answered. He had been so determinedly staring straight ahead that he was startled to see that she had turned to face him.

For the first time since she had recognized Nathan, Angel met his gaze without hesitation. Her eyes were full of chaos. They reminded him of the dark volatility of the storm clouds that sometimes tumbled, snapping and crackling, across the sky on hot days. And it made him angry.

Everything about her presence made him angry. For much of the past seven years, her memory had been a spark of light in overwhelming darkness. Ten-year-old Angel had been innocence in a world that had otherwise been colored by shame, depravity, and misery. Nathan could still feel, as sharply as he had that day, the sting of humiliation from watching his father be escorted from the saloon. In spite of this, he had clung to the memory of Angel, because the memory of Angel was a memory of a few moments without fear. Her memory was a reminder that someone, somewhere, had neither judged him nor expected him to pay for the sins of his father.

He had reminded himself of that every time a conversation abruptly stopped when he came too close, or when whispers followed him as he walked by, or when someone avoided meeting his eyes as they spoke. But now, the Angel from that memory was gone, ripped from him and destroyed. Innocence and hope had been replaced by something darker. The anxiety and tension he had been feeling before transformed into hostility, and the words he drawled out were cruel. "Angel. There's some irony for you."

Her expression turned cold. "I don't understand. What is that supposed to mean?"

Nathan smiled, but the expression was not kind. "I think it's pretty obvious."

"I don't think it is. Why don't you explain it to me?" Angel's tone was icy.

Nathan stared at her in disbelief, but her face was stony and unwavering, and he realized she was serious. He began speaking with exaggerated slowness, deliberate and antagonistic. "You lived and worked at the saloon."

"Yes." Angel nodded.

Nathan, already beginning to regret the direction he had steered this conversation, waited for Angel to say something, anything, so that he didn't have to, but when she said nothing, he continued in his deliberate drawl. "I had an interesting conversation with a man at the general store today. He likes to talk."

Angel turned to face him, and then with the air of one who knew what Nathan's answer to her question would be and how uncomfortable it would make him to speak it, Angel raised her chin. Almost daring him to answer, she asked, "And what exactly did he say?"

"He asked me how well I knew you. And then he said"—here Nathan took a deep breath, then spoke, his bitterness giving him renewed courage, mimicking the storekeeper's conspiratorial tone—"'Well, son, I'll tell you man to man—there's at least one man who knew her better than you.'"

Judging by her reddened cheeks, Angel took the storekeeper's meaning without trouble, as Nathan himself had, and Nathan asked a biting question. "Was that clear enough, or would you like me to explain some more?"

His satisfaction at Angel's stunned expression lasted only a moment, until Angel, who had been sitting straight-backed on the seat beside Nathan, wrapped her arms around her chest, hugging herself tightly like she was trying to hold herself together. She sat perfectly still, although her breathing was uneven, making it sound as though she were shivering.

Nathan had the uncomfortable feeling that the words he had spoken had been, if it were possible, far crueler than he had intended. Nathan waited for her to reply, and when she said nothing, he shook his head. The anger he had felt only moments earlier had burned itself out and replaced itself with an almost hollow lack of interest in anything Angel might say. He had inherited some of his father's temper, but not his temperament, and guilt for how he had spoken was starting to nudge at him.

Finally, after a long silence, Angel spoke, her voice scarcely above a whisper. "Some things don't happen by choice."

Some of Nathan's initial irritation flared up again, and he spat, "How was that not a choice?"

Angel stared intently at the floorboards, and then spoke one word. "Rape." She paused, then added, "Now is when you tell me that it was my fault."

Nathan felt the air leave his lungs in a single breath, and his mouth moved like a fish that had been caught and was now lying on the bank of the river, slowly suffocating.

Angel was still speaking. It sounded like she was reciting a list, and Nathan suspected it was a list that someone else—or several someone elses—had given her. "I shouldn't have been there. I shouldn't have worked in a saloon—this would never have happened to a proper lady. This is my punishment for associating with women of that nature. I shouldn't have done my hair that way, I shouldn't have worn that color, I should have fought harder. I must have brought it on myself. I must have wanted it to happen—"

"Stop." Nathan's voice was raised as he cut her off. Angel looked startled, searching his face with something that looked briefly like hope. All of Nathan's words dissolved in his mouth. He had not thought beyond stopping the pounding assault of her words.

Finally, he asked, "Is that what that man at the store was talking about? When he said another man knew you better? He was talking about you being raped?"

Nathan could barely choke out the last word. Angel didn't answer, but she shot him a look that plainly showed she thought the answer to Nathan's question should be obvious.

"Son of a—" Nathan started to swear, then paused, glancing at Angel. "Sorry," he muttered. Then, "Do you really believe all that—everything you said—that it's your fault?"

Angel shrugged, shaking her head almost imperceptibly. "Doesn't matter."

"Why doesn't it matter?"

"Everyone else believes it is."

RAPE. Angel didn't know what had caused her to speak that word, other than the knowledge that as soon as they reached the next fork in the road, they would part ways and she would never have to face Nathan again. That, and an anger-inspired desire to make Nathan feel as uncomfortable as she had. She had wanted to shock him, to make him flinch, and to deflect some of the embarrassment and shame she felt away from herself and back toward him.

So she had told the truth, but her truth was taboo, and now she wished she had never broken the silence.

Angel sighed and buried her face in her hands. Closing her eyes, she tried to calm her racing heart, letting the sounds of the wagon and horses and harness drift into background noise. She focused on the sound of her breathing, but with her eyes closed, it wasn't long before the motion of the wagon made her stomach queasy, and she sneaked a peek at Nathan out of the corner of her eye. He was staring straight ahead. He looked so uncomfortably miserable that a flash of amusement shocked her, and she had to cough to keep startled laughter from passing her lips.

At the sound of her cough, Nathan glanced toward Angel. As soon as their eyes met, Angel and Nathan looked away as though if they separated their eyes fast enough, they could erase the brief contact before it had ever happened.

Angel wished she had never accepted Nathan's help. Walking the several extra miles could never have been as painful as this wagon ride. After what seemed like an eternity, a small town came into view on the road ahead, and Nathan spoke.

"I'll take you to the preacher's house when we get into town. He and his wife are good folk—you'll be able to stay with them until you can make other arrangements."

When Angel was silent, he added gently, "Do you need money?"

Nathan's words ground against Angel's pride, sparking it to life. She raised her chin, her jaw tightening. "No."

Nathan exhaled, then said, "You'll be okay."

Angel nodded, wondering whether Nathan was trying to reassure her or himself. There was another long pause. They were surrounded by emptiness begging to be filled with accusations, or explanations, or apologies, or maybe all three, but Angel could think of nothing left to say. As she climbed down from the wagon, she wondered why, after so many wrong words, it was so hard to find one right word.

4

He was always the golden child, the chosen son. I was the oldest —it should have been me. But nothing I did was ever good enough.

THE LITTLE TOWN WAS QUIET, and the preacher's house even more so. Nathan walked Angel to the door, knocked, then waited. There was no answer. With a sinking feeling in his stomach, Nathan knocked once more, harder this time. Still no answer. He turned to see a woman from the house across the street watching them.

"If you're looking for the preacher and his wife—" the woman started, and Nathan wondered who else he and Angel could possibly have been looking for, knocking on the preacher's door—"they've left."

"Do you know when they'll be back?"

"They won't. They announced in church a few weeks back that they were moving on. You must not have been at church that Sunday."

Nathan closed his eyes and sighed, then turned to Angel. "Guess we'll try the hotel then."

Angel nodded mutely, then walked with Nathan back to the wagon. This time she didn't see—or she ignored—the hand Nathan extended to help her climb up into the seat.

The hotel—if it could be called such—was located above the general store and was comprised of a few spare rooms the owners occasionally rented out to travelers. It was small and simple, but it was also clean and respectable.

Nathan and Angel walked into the general store, and Nathan groaned inwardly as he saw the young woman standing behind the counter. Valentine. Her parents owned the store and the hotel, but Valentine sometimes stood in for her parents.

Valentine's eyes moved back and forth between Nathan and Angel before settling on Angel with a cool gaze. After a moment, Angel looked down at the counter, her hands twisting as she fidgeted. Nathan broke the silence. "Do you have a room available for the night?"

Turning her gaze toward Nathan, Valentine smiled. "I'm sorry, but we do not."

Nathan scrubbed at his face as he tried to hide his irritation. He couldn't be sure, but he had a strong hunch that there were rooms available—they just weren't available for Angel. He opened his mouth to argue with Valentine, but Angel stopped him with a shake of her head.

"Never mind, Nathan. Let's go."

Nathan could feel Valentine's gaze boring into them from behind as they exited the building. Once they were outside, Nathan shook his head and, speaking more to himself than to Angel, he asked aloud, "Now what?"

The silence hung in the air for several moments, and then Angel spoke. "You should go."

Nathan turned to look at her, protesting, "I'm not leaving until I know you have somewhere to go."

Angel crossed her arms against her chest. "It will be easier for me to find somewhere to stay if you aren't with me."

Stung, Nathan turned from Angel to look back toward the store they had just come from. A shadow—Valentine—quickly ducked out of sight. Nathan gritted his teeth as his frustration threatened to boil over. He didn't need this.

"Fine," he said, acid and ice dripping from his words. "I apologize for inconveniencing you. I didn't realize my company was so distasteful."

He tipped his hat at Angel, then climbed into the wagon. As he lifted the reins, he glanced at back Angel, standing motionless beside the wagon. Confusion passed over her face, and her eyebrows pinched together. She seemed like she might say something, but when she remained silent, Nathan shook his head and clucked his tongue at the horse.

NATHAN SAT NEXT to his father on the seat of the wagon. The hours of the ride home had been filled with welcome silence, but Nathan knew better than to hope it meant anything other than a beating to look forward to when they arrived home. His father was brooding.

The silence was uneasy, like the quiet that came before a storm. The difference was that during a bad storm, you could go underground. Nathan had yet to find anywhere to hide from his father. He had been nine the first time he had run away, and his father had caught up with him the same day. Nathan had run away three times since then, and every time, his father had found him. The last time, his father had beaten him so badly that, in the words of his father, there "weren't no way the boy could run now, even if he got the notion to try."

Nathan hadn't tried running since.

When they arrived home, his father went inside without a word to Nathan. Nathan did his chores in silence. Even more than the inevitable beating, he hated the uncertainty of the wait. It would have been one thing if there had been hope that his father's mood would blow over, but there wasn't. His father was the master, and Nathan was the proverbial dog that had been kicked—over and over again.

Nathan felt a strange sense of relief as he finished the last of the chores and closed the barn door for the night. In his mind's eye, he could envision his father standing, belt in hand, in the middle of the floor, and yet he felt some of the tension ease out of his body. There was no more fear that his father would surprise him from behind while he was milking the cow or pitching hay down from the loft. Only the sure knowledge that once he entered the cabin, the worst would happen and then be over.

But when he walked through the front door, his father wasn't standing in the middle of the room as Nathan had anticipated. Before Nathan could look around, his father, who must have been waiting just inside the door, grabbed his shirt collar, yanking him sideways and off balance, and then pushed him backward against the wall.

"I don't want no son of mine whoring after them women."

His father's words were still slurred, and his face was so close Nathan could smell the reek of alcohol on his breath. Not that that was saying much —the smell of alcohol on his father was so strong Nathan would have been able to smell it from across the room.

Nathan stared at his father, his disbelief twofold. Aside from the utter hypocrisy of the statement, the fact that his father would even insinuate that ten-year-old Angel was some kind of prostitute—and that he, Nathan, had been "whoring after" her—made his insides turn over on themselves. He couldn't keep a look of disgust from rising to his face.

Nathan spoke out of shock, rather than a desire to argue. "She's not a whore, and I wasn't—"

His father interrupted him, his voice filled with contempt. "All women are whores. You'll learn, and then you'll know, just like me."

The words flew out of Nathan's mouth before he could stop them. "I will never," he spat out, "be anything like you."

He expected his words to infuriate his father, but instead, they had the opposite effect. His father stepped back, releasing Nathan's shoulders from his grasp as he did so, his hands falling to his sides.

A cold smile spread over his father's face, and he laughed before he spoke. "Boy, it's in your blood. You are me. You just don't know it yet."

NATHAN THOUGHT he would feel relieved as he and Angel separated to go their own ways, but instead, he felt worse. A strange anxiety he couldn't quite describe started at the base of his skull, and then crept outward from there, filling his mind, twisting his stomach, and tightening his hold on the reins.

The shock of meeting Angel on the road had unsettled Nathan. Even though he had stopped in the general store to ask what had become of Angel, Nathan had never truly expected to see her again. Angel's town was not so far from where he lived, but it was far enough that either Angel or Nathan would have had to go out of their way for their paths to cross again. Angel wouldn't have known how to find him, even if she had wanted to. And until his father had left for good, Nathan had never thought about going back.

Well, that wasn't quite true. He had thought about it, once. That thought had been quashed with the realization that by doing so, he would create one more thread tying Angel's life to his—and correspondingly, to his father's. Nathan had been able to think of nothing worse.

But his father was gone now.

Nathan played his and Angel's conversation over and over in his mind, trying to reason away the sinking feeling in his stomach. Angel had asked—no, insisted—that Nathan leave. He had left. That was all there was to it. So why did he feel like he was going to be sick?

Nathan had unhitched the horses from the wagon and finished rubbing them down, and was measuring out the grain in their stalls before he finally made his decision. He grabbed a bridle off the wall and slid it onto the mare's nose when she lifted her head out of the bucket, chewing a mouthful of oats. She tossed her head, protesting the idea of leaving her meal.

"Easy," Nathan soothed her, patting her neck. "We'll be right back, I promise."

The mare eyed him, then shoved her nose back in the bucket for another mouthful of oats. He pulled at the bridle, and, shaking her head, she grudgingly followed him back out of the barn. He lifted himself up onto her back—he didn't bother with a saddle—and they set out. The mare had a long stride that was smooth and covered ground quickly; it didn't take long for the town to reappear in the distance, and once there, it took even less time for Nathan to find Angel.

She was sitting on the front steps of the saloon.

Still far enough away to have escaped Angel's notice, Nathan pulled back on the reins and slid off the mare without speaking. Nathan stood, silently watching Angel, and a strange feeling that he had been in this moment before passed through him. Just like the first day they had met, Nathan felt himself drawn to her. He walked slowly toward her, pausing to wrap the reins of the bridle around the hitching post, then sat heavily down beside her. Angel hastily scrubbed at her eyes, and, with a realization that made his stomach twist into an even tighter knot, Nathan saw that she had been crying.

"Why are you here, Nathan?" Angel asked.

"I wanted to make sure you had a place to stay."

Angel laughed softly, without humor. "Turns out there isn't a place for someone like me."

Even though Nathan knew Angel was simply responding to what he had said, he had the uncomfortable feeling that Angel's response meant something more: that there was no place, anywhere, for her. They sat in silence for a few moments, and then Nathan gestured at the building they sat in front of. "The saloon?" he asked.

Angel shot him a look of disgust. "I'm not staying at the saloon."

"No," Nathan said. "I mean, why are you sitting in front of the saloon?"

Angel was quiet for so long Nathan thought she wouldn't answer, but she finally said, "Maybe this is where I belong. Maybe I never should have left the saloon. People look at me the same no matter where I'm at, but at least before I wasn't trying to be anything different."

Nathan snorted, and Angel looked at him in surprise. "You don't believe that," he said.

"Don't I?"

"No. At least, not all of it."

Angel held his gaze for a moment—not agreeing, but not arguing —before resting her chin on her hand and staring down the road toward the general store. "That girl at the store—she doesn't seem to like me much."

"Yeah, Valentine's a real piece of work."

"That's one way to put it," Angel muttered.

A smile flitted across Nathan's face, then fled as Angel heaved a sigh and leaned forward to lay her head on her arms, crossed and resting on her knees. She didn't have to speak to let Nathan know what she was thinking. The edge of the sun was just beginning to touch the horizon, and soon it would be dark. And Angel still had no place to stay. Unless . . .

No. That was a terrible idea.

But Nathan was out of good ideas.

He glanced again at the setting sun, then turned to Angel and blurted, "Stay with me."

His words were meant as a question, but Angel's face paled. The words that tumbled from her lips were rushed, as though her hasty explanation could form a physical barrier between them. "No. It's not—I can't. Please, just leave. I never worked there, not like that . . ." Her words trailed off as Nathan, realizing what she thought he was asking of her, raised his hands, palms out, and hastily reassured her.

"I know."

The panic in her eyes faded, but she continued to stare at him, unsure, and she leaned away from him, her arms folded across her chest, fingernails digging into her skin. Nathan held himself perfectly still, afraid to push nerves that had already been stretched, barely moving his mouth as he spoke, glancing around to make sure no one was near enough to overhear their conversation.

"I know you didn't work at the saloon like that. I'm not asking you to stay *with* me—not in that way at least. But right now you don't have anywhere else to go. I don't want anything in return. You helped me

once. Let me repay the favor. Stay with me until you can find something better."

Angel's body slowly untensed as he spoke, but when she
replied there was a bitter edge to her voice. "When we met, when I
helped you before—that was innocence. I was ten years old. It's
been seven years since—almost a whole other lifetime. I'm not the
same."

He spoke slowly. "It meant everything to me at the time. Let me
help you."

She shook her head. "I can't stay with you."

"Why?" Nathan asked.

"I just can't," she answered.

"If you can look me in the eyes and tell me you have any idea
where you are going, or what you will do until you get there, I won't
ask you again."

When she remained silent, he spoke again. "Stay. Just for a day or
two, until you have a better plan. Besides, there will be a train coming
through in a couple days."

Still, Angel hesitated, looking at Nathan as though he were
missing the most obvious problem in the world. "Aren't you afraid of
what people will say?"

His bark of self-deprecating laughter caught her off guard. "I'm
the son of an abusive drunk of a father who disappears for months at
a time and hasn't been seen now for over a year. I'm used to what
people say." He paused, then spoke the word one more time, gently:
"Stay."

ANGEL'S EYES flickered away from Nathan, then back, and then away
again. She was accustomed to the things people whispered when she
walked by, but the words never stung less. Still, she had never
expected the cruelty that Nathan had shown, the way he had spat her
name like it was dirty. Nathan's words had pierced even through the
walls of Angel's expectations to score their marks on her heart. But

now, he was offering her a place to stay, and twin emotions warred inside her.

Her heart couldn't help feeling a sudden twinge of relief, but her mind couldn't help balking at the pull of the idea.

The silence lengthened, growing more and more uncomfortable until Angel finally blurted, "Why?"

"Why?" Nathan repeated, surprised.

"Yes. Why are you offering me a place to stay, and how would it even be possible, and—" Angel paused. Her voice was half a tone lower as she continued. "And when you wake up tomorrow morning, will you wish you could pretend today was only a dream, or will you want to believe that it was real?"

Nathan considered her for a long moment. Angel held her breath, waiting.

"If I wake up tomorrow morning and this is real, what of it? Whether it is or isn't, I don't want you to leave. I'm asking you to stay because if I don't, I'll regret it. As for how it would be possible, that's up to you. If you want to stay, it'll be possible. If you don't"—Nathan shrugged—"it won't be."

"But why do you want me to stay?" Angel pressed.

Again, Nathan didn't respond immediately. When he did, it didn't appear to be in response to her question. "I'm sorry for everything— for what I said earlier, for leaving you here in town, for what happened to you. I'm sorry for it all."

"You want me to stay because you feel sorry for me?" Angel interpreted. Her insides cringed, and she was sure her expression reflected her distaste.

"Nah." Nathan's voice softened. "I want you to stay because I care what happens to you. Like I said, you helped me. Let me help you."

Angel was silent for a long moment, then hesitantly, she asked, "I helped you? But what did I do that anyone else wouldn't have done?"

Nathan searched Angel's face, a bemused look on his own as though he didn't understand why she would ask a question to which the answer was so obvious. Finally, with a slight shrug and a half smile, he answered, "Everything."

Angel pondered his words, then spoke. "You didn't truly leave me in town. You came back."

A faint smile passed across Nathan's lips. "There is that," he admitted.

"So?" Nathan asked. Angel knew what he meant, even though he had left the real question unspoken. She wouldn't make him repeat what he had already asked her so many times. She took a deep breath —she felt like she was jumping off a cliff blind, hoping that water or wings would break her fall—and answered, "Yes, I will stay."

5

Even after I saved my brother's life, I couldn't do any right in my father's eyes. The day I saved my brother, my father beat me worse than he ever had—he said all because I nearly let my fool brother get himself killed.

ANGEL LOOKED AT THE MARE. "Should I ride behind you or . . ."

Her words trailed off and Nathan rubbed the back of his neck, recognizing for the first time the problems the lone, saddleless horse and Angel's long skirts presented to propriety. Nathan ran through several possibilities in his mind, immediately discarding any scenario that involved Angel's arms around him, or his around her, and settled on the only option he could think of that remained.

"You can ride, and I'll walk," Nathan said. Angel looked as though she might protest, so he quickly added, "The mare's tired. She'll be glad to be carrying only one of us anyway."

To Nathan's relief, Angel nodded. She walked to where Nathan was standing, and he cupped his hands together so that Angel could step into them and he could boost her onto the mare's back.

As Nathan moved to lift Angel onto the horse, he paused, looking around to the nearly empty street and handful of people who were trying—and failing—to look as though they were not paying Nathan and Angel the slightest attention.

"Maybe we should wait until we are outside of town to ride."

Angel followed Nathan's gaze down the length of the street, then shook her head. "If we walk to the edge of town, it will look like we are trying to hide something."

Nathan shrugged, then stooped and cupped his hands again.

Just as Nathan had lifted Angel onto the horse and handed her the reins, a voice hailed them. The soft dirt of the road had muffled the sound of someone approaching, and Nathan had been too preoccupied with settling Angel on the horse to notice anyone nearby.

Nathan turned at the sound of the voice, and the rider raised his hand to touch the brim of his hat. "Nathan."

The greeting was a statement, but the man watched Angel as he spoke, and Nathan heard the question behind the man's salute. Nathan looked at Angel, noticing her legs for the first time since he had lifted her astride the horse, bare up to her knees.

"Carl," Nathan returned the man's greeting, drawing his attention.

"You're in town late," Carl observed, his eyes still on Angel.

"We were just leaving," Nathan answered, keeping his reply short.

Carl raised an eyebrow, nodding thoughtfully as he spoke. "Well, I'd best let you get on your way. You'll want to make it to wherever you're heading before dark."

Ignoring the implied question, Nathan nodded, touched the brim of his hat, and patted the mare's neck. "All right, Lady. Let's go home." The horse snorted, as though to remind Nathan that leaving had not been her idea and started off in her long gait.

When they had left the man and the town out of sight, Angel spoke. "That man, Carl, do you know him well?"

Nathan shrugged. "Well enough. He owns the general store here in town. And he's Valentine's father."

"Is he much like Valentine?"

"She had to learn it somewhere."

"He and Valentine—they'll tell people they saw us together?" Angel asked, but Nathan knew it was more a statement of fact than a question.

"Yes."

Angel sighed. "I left to get away from everyone who thought they knew something about me." She shook her head. "The stories are just following me."

Keeping his eyes on the road ahead, Nathan spoke. "There's something that I've been wondering about."

Nathan could almost feel Angel tense, but her voice was even as she responded, "Yes?"

"The man at the general store back in your town—he said you left days ago. How is it you ended up on the side of the road as I was passing by?"

Angel shook her head, looking annoyed. "I didn't leave until today. Geoffrey, the store owner, likes to think he knows everything. I bought a few things at the store he thought were suspicious—he was quite nosy about it—so when he didn't see me for a couple days, he must have figured I had already left."

Nathan did not respond for a long moment, then asked, "Why didn't you leave sooner?"

Angel smoothed the mare's mane along the horse's neck, considering Nathan's question before she answered. Finally, she said, "I was . . . rather ill in the months after the attack, and I didn't have anywhere else to go. When I began to feel well enough to leave the saloon for longer periods, I started to hear the things people were saying about me—about the attack—and I knew I couldn't stay any longer. I stopped caring that I didn't know where I was going—I just wanted to be someplace where nobody knew who I was."

Nathan glanced back at Angel over his shoulder, waiting for her to continue, but when she did not, he sighed and turned his attention to the road ahead and to the clouds overhead, slowly fading from pink and gold to red and orange, then deep purple and blue. Silence again surrounded Nathan and Angel as they traveled, but this time the silence was quiet and still rather than harsh and piercing. They had made their way nearly back to the farm, the first star just appearing in the night sky, when Angel realized what had been missing from their conversation. As they rounded the bend and the farmstead came into view, she asked abruptly, "What about your father?"

Nathan's hands tightened on the reins. "He's gone," he said shortly.

"Gone?" Angel asked. "Gone where? When will he be back?"

Nathan watched her out of the corner of his eye as he spoke. "I don't know where he's gone, but I doubt he'll be coming back."

"How do you know?" Angel pressed.

Nathan grimaced. "My father used to disappear for weeks, sometimes months, at a time. Usually during the winter. But this spring he never came back, and a few months ago the sheriff came by, saying my father was suspected of killing a man, asking if I'd seen him or knew where he went."

"Your father killed someone?" Angel whispered.

Nathan shrugged. "Probably. I haven't seen or heard from him since. I reckon I won't, either. He knows I have no reason to keep his secrets."

"Who was it? Do you know why?"

Nathan shook his head. "Nah, the sheriff didn't say much else. And I didn't ask. As bad as it sounds, it's probably not the first time he's killed someone."

There was finality in Nathan's last statement. Angel could feel him waiting for her reaction, but she was unsettled, and unsure how to respond. Her unease stemmed more from Nathan's cavalier attitude than from his father's actions. Of the two, it was Nathan's attitude that seemed more out of place. Finally, when she could avoid it no longer, Angel asked, "Don't you care?"

Nathan laughed without humor. "Don't I care about what? My father being gone? My father killing someone?"

Angel shrugged apologetically as she answered, "Both."

Nathan sighed. As he turned toward her, his eyes were tired, and Angel caught a glimpse of the same shame and sadness she had seen in the boy she had known years ago. "Yes, I care. I hate everything about who my father is and what he's done, but I can't change either of those things. I learned a long time ago that I can't blame myself for all the things my father's done. If I did, I think I'd've given up a long time ago."

Abruptly, Nathan's tone changed and he gestured to the building in front of them. Almost without Angel realizing it, they had come to a stop in front of the small cabin they had gradually been approaching.

"You can sleep inside tonight. I'll sleep in the loft of the barn." He shook his head as Angel opened her mouth to protest. "It's not far enough into fall to be cold at night yet, and the barn holds warmth well, especially with the animals inside. I'll be fine." His tone held the certainty of knowledge, and Angel suspected he had spent more than a few nights in the barn loft in years past.

Angel hesitantly approached the cabin door. As she raised her hand to push the door open, she looked over her shoulder at Nathan, but he was already leading the mare to the barn, his back toward her. She raised the latch on the door, pushed it open, and stepped inside.

The room was dim, the last vestiges of the fading daylight filtering through a small, west-facing window. A wooden table stood in the middle of the room, flanked by two chairs. On the table was a lamp, which Angel lit. The light that blossomed from the flame flickered on the walls and warmed the room with a welcoming glow.

With the increased light, Angel's attention was drawn to more details—a fireplace to the right, pots and pans stacked on shelves against the back wall, a mattress pushed up against the wall near the fire, and a door leading to a back room.

The back room was empty, except for a large mattress. She paced nervously around the table in the first room, then sat, then stood again, all the while watching the front door, unsure of what to do. In the end, it was the tiredness that made the decision for her.

The chair drew her in first—a welcome relief to her aching feet. She unlaced her boots and gingerly removed them, and then her stockings. There were blisters on her feet, but she breathed a sigh of relief to see that none of them had broken, although a few had come close. Then, as she sat, elbows leaned against the table, head in her hands, the flickering flame of the lamp lowered her eyelids. They were so heavy.

It wasn't until her chin slipped off of her cupped hand and her head jerked toward the table that the spell of the lamp was broken. And then she stopped caring which bed she should choose or what Nathan might think. All she wanted was to let her exhausted body sleep. Angel made her way to a room, a bed. She barely had time to offer a silent prayer heavenward, *Lord keep us safe*, and then she was asleep.

HER BODY FELT HEAVY, her lungs thick, slow—like they did when she dreamed she was underwater. It was dark, not because there was no light, but because she couldn't force her eyelids to open more than a crack. As she slowly floated to the surface, back to consciousness, the sound of the slightest breath escaped her lips, and she turned her head. With her movement came the sound of shattered glass crunching against the wood floor. She was on the floor—how did she get on the floor? Her eyes flickered open. There was so much glass. She could feel it pressing into her hair, stinging against her skull. There was blood on the glass. She didn't know if it was hers. Every part of her body hurt.

Suddenly, some of the weight lifted off her, and she realized the heaviness she had felt had not been entirely because of her unconsciousness. Her stomach remembered before her mind did, and she found herself retching on the floor as the memories came back in flashes—a single gunshot, one man collapsing, another man leering, her head smashing into the glass mirror behind the bar, bottles breaking and alcohol running down the wall and onto the floor. Fading consciousness, hands on her shoulders, pushing her down. And then, a weight. A weight so heavy it made it hard to breathe.

Her body had hurt then—her throat raw from a silent scream, her muscles bruised from hands that held too tight and wooden corners and edges and lines that didn't give, her skin stinging from glass shards, her chest caving in on itself knowing that Tom, her uncle, was dead. But now, as the weight lifted from her, there was a new pain.

As the last of the unconsciousness left her, she was finally able to open her eyes, knowing what would greet her. The man stood in front of her, but he was only a dark silhouette against the light of the window. Even without seeing his expression, she could feel the leer stretch across his face as her eyes opened. Then, as if he hadn't done enough, he left her with one parting stroke. "Angel, no more," he breathed.

And then he turned and walked out the door.

ANGEL WOKE SCREAMING. Somehow, the voice she could never find in her nightmares always found her in the waking moments. At first it had seemed strange to her, the juxtaposition of wakeful and night-marish reality, but as time passed and the nightmares continued, she had slowly realized that even when she was awake, the nightmare was her reality. After that, it no longer seemed so strange. Only cold.

She shuddered with a chill that came from inside, not out, and pulled the blankets up around her ears and rolled back to her side. A frantic pounding on the door sent another jolt of fear and adrenaline rushing through her body.

"Angel, are you all right?" Nathan's anxious voice reached her through the door.

"Yes," she tried to reply, but the whisper she managed didn't have a chance of being heard over the sound of his hand against the door.

"Angel?" Nathan asked more loudly. The pounding on the door escalated. Angel sighed and, wrapping the blankets around herself, walked to the door.

"Yes," she tried again. This time, the sound that escaped her throat was a hoarse croak, but Nathan heard her, and the pounding on the door stopped. There was a brief pause, then, "What happened?" Nathan asked. His voice was slightly calmer, but still held an edge.

"I'm fine," Angel reassured him, although she knew no amount of reassurance was likely to counteract the effect of waking up to screams in the middle of the night. "I just . . . I have nightmares sometimes."

"Oh." Nathan was silent, then said, "I have those sometimes too."

"What about?" As soon as Angel asked the question, she wished she could take it back. It was too close. She wasn't sure she would have wanted to answer if he had asked her the same, and besides, she could already guess what he would say.

Angel heard Nathan exhale deeply on the other side of the door. Then came a soft thud and the sound of heavy fabric sliding against wood, like he had leaned his back against the door and then slid down against it to sit on the floor. Angel copied his movements and slid down to sit with her back against the door. It felt closer—warmer —sitting this way, back to back, even with the hardwood between them. She was grateful for the distance provided by the door. Somehow it made the closeness feel safer. The shivers that had held her since she had woken slowly relaxed their grip.

"Sometimes I dream about my father," Nathan answered her question. "When I was younger, I'd have nightmares about my father coming home drunk and beating me. I could never get away. Now, I have dreams where my father is hurting someone else, and I can't do anything to stop it. Sometimes I think it's my mother. Sometimes I think it's just a younger version of myself. Once . . ." Nathan paused, and the drawn-out silence was painful. He continued, and admitted, "Once it was you."

"Me?" Angel was startled. She was glad he couldn't see her eyebrows pinch together from the other side of the door. "Why me?"

Nathan chuckled faintly, but without humor. *Someday*, Angel thought, *I would like to hear that sound when there is really laughter behind it.*

"It was a while after we had met the first time. You were so different from anyone I had ever known. You were the only person I'd met who didn't judge me by my father's actions.

"One night my father got drunk and beat me the worst I think he ever has. I was so sick that night. I was lying there on the bed, and swearing to myself that as soon as I got better I was going to run, to leave for good. I remembered you, and what you had done the last time my father had hit me when my back was all tore up, and how it had stopped hurting—how I had stopped hurting. I couldn't stop thinking about you, and then my father came in and sat down beside me and said, 'Nathan, what would I do without you?' I didn't answer, just kept staring at the wall, and he just kept looking at me. Finally, I said, 'I don't know, I guess you'd have to find someone else to knock around.' And then he laughed, and he said, 'That's right, son. I guess I would.' Then he went and brought the doctor—told him I'd got bucked off a horse. When my father left the room and I heard him say, 'He's all yours, doc,' and the doctor came in. He knew my father was lying—wouldn't look me in the eye the whole time he was there.

"Anyhow, the point is, that night was the first night I dreamed about my father that he wasn't hurting me. He was hurting someone else—you—and I couldn't do anything about it except watch, because I wasn't really there."

Angel didn't know what to say, other than to ask the question that was on the tip of her tongue. "Is that why you've stayed—to keep your father from hurting someone else?"

In the silence, she could almost hear him shrug on the other side of the door. "Maybe."

There was a pause, then Nathan continued. "After that night, things changed. I changed—I wasn't scared anymore. I think my father knew something was different. It was right after that he started leaving. At first, it was just a day or two at a time. Then toward the end, he would leave for weeks at a time. Now . . ." Nathan's voice trailed off, and Angel finished the sentence for him.

"Now he's gone."

"Now he's gone," Nathan echoed, then continued. "The only times I've thought of leaving were when my father was here. But now, I've put more sweat into this place than he ever thought about. I've made this place mine in every way that matters, and now it's mine by law.

"When I was young, I used to dream of escaping from my father. It's been a long time since I've been afraid of him though."

Angel wrapped the blanket more tightly around herself. As she did, a faint glow caught her eye. It was barely there, the scrap of light, leftover like bread crumbs brushed from the kitchen table, straggling from the west window to find its way through the gap between the wood floor and bottom of the door. The glow was more of a lesser darkness than anything else, but she had been sitting in the blackness for so long that even that faint glimmer stood out.

"It's getting light outside," she observed out loud.

"You should go back to sleep and get some rest," Nathan said. He shifted, and it sounded like he was standing.

"What about you?" Angel asked quickly. She could feel the brief closeness they had shared start to evaporate, and she wanted to hold on to it for as long as possible.

"It's about time I was up anyway," Nathan answered. "I've got plenty to do today."

"Can I help?" Angel asked.

Nathan didn't answer right away. When he did, there was finality in his tone. "You can rest."

"Nathan?" Angel raised her voice in question one last time. When she heard him pause his movements outside the door, she asked, "Why did you tell me this tonight?"

There was silence as Nathan considered his response. Finally, he spoke. "Everyone knows about my father. That's nothing new. As for the rest of it . . . I suppose sometimes it's easier to trade secrets in darkness than daylight."

Angel waited for him to continue, but all he said was "Get some rest, Angel." She heard the sound of footsteps on the wooden floor, the front door squeaking as it opened and closed, and then, once more, silence. Her eyes were heavy as she crawled back into bed, but this time, she knew she would sleep without nightmares. Nathan was gone, but the feeling of safety remained, surrounding her until she drifted into dreamless sleep.

6

Maybe saving my brother was my first mistake.

THE NEXT MORNING, Angel awoke to the feeling of coarse fabric pressing against her cheek. Sleep departed slowly, and as her awareness grew, her senses were torn between startled unfamiliarity and the enveloping comfort of the bed. The crack of light underneath the bedroom door had brightened to a dim glow. A muffled and rhythmic *thunk, thunk* came from outside, and curiosity pulled her from beneath the covers. She dressed quickly and followed the sound to the back of the cabin.

Nathan was splitting firewood. His movements were smooth, practiced. He grinned as he saw Angel come around the corner of the cabin. It was an action so ordinary that it caught Angel off guard.

Are we going to pretend that what we are doing is normal? Angel thought, but in spite of her misgivings, she found herself grinning back.

Today, she thought with an inward smile, *today, we will pretend.*

NATHAN LOOKED up from the stump where he was splitting firewood to see Angel walk around the corner of the cabin. He smiled at her, and as she smiled back, he remembered the question she had asked a day earlier—when you wake up, will you want to pretend this is all a dream, or will you want to believe it is real?

He turned back to his work, the worn wood of the axe sliding across his palm as he swung it over and down, over and down. Finally, as the axe settled into the wooden stump with a *thunk* and Nathan turned to walk toward Angel, wiping his hands on his pants, his mind wandered over the events from the day before. He sat down across from her with the sun kissing the tops of their heads and the dew carrying the sweet smells of earth and grass upward as it evaporated, and he couldn't help thinking that in spite of the nightmares of the night before, or maybe because of them, this morning seemed more dream than reality. But he wanted it to be real.

They sat in silence for a moment until their eyes met, and then Nathan spoke the first thing that came to mind. "How'd you sleep?" he asked.

"Fine, thank you."

"Any more nightmares?"

"No."

"I'm glad." Nathan started to stand, but Angel interrupted him.

"I want to help while I'm here."

Her eyes were earnest, almost pleading, and Nathan thought he understood what Angel hadn't spoken—it was better to be busy than to be left with too much time to think. Being left alone with one's thoughts was sometimes dangerous.

Nathan sighed at her persistence, then smiled and offered her a hand to help her stand. "All right, let's see what we can find for you to do around here."

As Angel stood, Nathan mentally scanned the cabin and surrounding property. Now that his father was gone, Nathan was accustomed to keeping up with the work himself. He didn't want to ask more of Angel than she was capable of—he didn't know if she knew anything about the day-to-day chores that Nathan took for granted—but he also suspected she wouldn't take kindly to being assigned a task simply to keep her busy.

In the end, he settled on having her help with what he had already planned to do that day—restuff the mattresses in the cabin and move one of the mattresses out to the barn. He had cut grass for hay two days prior. The weather had been sunny and warm since, so he expected the hay would be fully dried.

They gathered armfuls of sweet-smelling hay until the mattresses were full. As Angel stuffed the last of the hay into the mattress, Nathan caught himself staring at her slightly flushed cheeks and the strands of hair that had escaped her long, dark braid to cling damply to her forehead in the humidity. Angel noticed his gaze and self-consciously lifted a hand to the side of her face.

"Is something wrong?" she asked anxiously.

"No, no, nothing is wrong," he hastily reassured her, and she uncertainly resumed fastening the buttons on the end of the mattress. He snuck one last glance at her before joining her. Even amid the darkness, and frustration, and exhaustion of the day before, Angel had been pretty. Today, in the sunlight and with the task at hand to distract her from darker thoughts, she was beautiful.

"There." Angel sat back as she finished the last of the buttons. "That's the last of it. Shall we hurry and take them back?" She glanced upward. "It feels like it is going to rain."

Nathan nodded, looking at the clouds gathering above. "I think you're right. The leaves are starting to turn over, anyway."

He shouldered the first mattress—it was more cumbersome than heavy—and together he and Angel began making their way back toward the cabin, walking easily in silence.

After Nathan had deposited the first mattress in the cabin, he left Angel to make up the bed, and set off at a jog to retrieve the second mattress before the storm hit. He couldn't help stopping to inhale deeply when he hit the edge of the meadow.

The wind was starting to pick up, bringing the scent of rain, and something sharper, with it.

A troubled Angel was waiting for him when he arrived back at the cabin. "Nathan," she interrupted him as he carried the mattress to the barn. He turned to face her. Gone was the weightless girl from earlier in the afternoon. That light had faded with the sunlight, replaced by the storm clouds within and above. He smiled sadly, but Angel didn't notice. She was twisting her hands and didn't seem to know where to look.

"The barn, does it leak?" she asked anxiously.

Nathan was startled. "Well, I guess I've never slept there when it was raining before," he hastily reassured her as her brows furrowed, "but the cows have never complained, and anyway, I just patched the roof this summer. It'll be fine."

Angel nodded slowly, but she didn't seem convinced.

"It'll be fine," Nathan repeated. "Really."

When Angel didn't respond he grinned and jerked his head toward the barn. "Let me get this mattress down, and then we can have something to eat. Maybe after that I'll teach you how to milk a cow."

As Nathan strolled toward the barn under the load of the mattress, Angel couldn't help comparing the twelve-year-old boy she had met years ago with the person he had become. Yes, Nathan was taller, the angles of his face stronger. Those things had come with time. But he was more different than even seven years would have warranted under normal circumstances.

Angel remembered the twelve-year-old Nathan well—he was the youngest person besides herself she had seen at the saloon before or since. He had spent most of the time she had sat with him staring at the dust at his feet. Now, gone were the hunched shoulders, the jittery over-the-shoulder glances, and, perhaps most noticeably, the downcast eyes. Nathan didn't look down anymore.

What had changed? Angel wondered as she walked back to the cabin. She sometimes still felt like the little girl that had sat on the steps beside Nathan that day.

By the time Nathan had finished in the barn, the wind was howling against the cabin walls, and when Angel looked out the window, she could see tiny flakes of snow violently hurtling sideways through the air. She pressed the back of her hand against the glass and shuddered.

A gust of cold air blew in with Nathan, and he shook himself as he closed the door, stamping his feet and rubbing his hands together. He hadn't been dressed for the sudden drop in temperature.

"I'm glad you kept the fire going." Nathan nodded toward the fireplace and moved to stand in front of it.

"You were gone longer than I thought you would be."

"It started feeling cooler and the wind started picking up while I was putting the mattress up, so I decided to go ahead and milk the cow a bit earlier this evening. I'm glad I did. It's getting cold out there. Early winter storm, I guess."

Angel couldn't keep the concern from showing on her face, and Nathan hastily added, "I'll be warm enough."

Their meal was a silent affair. Angel used her spoon to push the food into patterns on her plate, and Nathan chewed in thoughtful silence. Both occasionally glanced at the window whenever a particularly strong gust of wind rattled the pane.

The contrast between the soft crackle of the warm flame and the constant, muted bluster of the cold outside made Angel shiver. Once, she saw Nathan anxiously watching the storm, but when he caught her eye, he merely smiled and shook his head, as though suggesting whatever his anxiety had been was nothing.

As the storm wore on, Angel grew more and more agitated. Storms made her nervous. They were unpredictable and had an uncanny knack for hiding things that, in her opinion, would have been better off remaining seen. It was cold outside, and no matter how many complaints Nathan assured her the cows did not have, she was sure the barn would not hold enough heat for him to stay warm all night.

Her thoughts drifted to their conversation from the night before, and she mused on what Nathan had said—it's easier to trade secrets in darkness than daylight. *It's true*, Angel thought, *because in the darkness you don't have to see yourself through the mirror of someone else's response.* But why trade secrets at all?

Nathan had spoken so easily to her that Angel felt a twinge of guilt for having offered nothing in return. Nothing voluntarily, at any rate. Nonetheless, she was grateful for what he had told her. It made her feel less of a burden and more of a friend.

Still, there was the matter of the barn.

No matter her uncertainty regarding Nathan in general, she could guess his response to the idea that had begun circling her thoughts as the evening progressed. Their current situation was not one of particular propriety, but she suspected that even so, Nathan would balk at what she was about to suggest.

Angel closed her eyes, pretending it was dark, and blurted, "Maybe you should stay inside tonight."

Nathan looked shocked, and he emphatically shook his head. "No," he spoke firmly. "It wouldn't be proper."

"How would that be different? Nothing about any of this"—Angel waved her arm inclusively—"is proper."

Nathan didn't argue as she had expected. Instead he shook his head and said, "You're right. It's not. I'm sorry for that. You deserve better."

Angel was taken aback by what Nathan had said, but before she could respond, another gust of wind shook the windowpane and Angel gestured toward it. "You are going to freeze outside."

Nathan merely shrugged. "I'll be fine."

Angel sighed with something that was not quite irritation and not quite admiration, but somewhere in between. She found herself watching him earnestly. This was made easier by the fact that Nathan seemed determined to avoid eye contact after Angel had suggested he stay inside, and had busied himself carving a small piece of wood into a shape that was yet to be uncovered. No matter what he said, he did not appear eager to brave the cold outside.

Angel closed her eyes, forcing herself to breath slowly, fighting to calm the rapidly increasing pounding of her heart before it choked out her breath altogether. Her tongue felt thick, heavy, clumsy. "You don't understand."

Finally, slightly exasperated, Nathan turned fully to face her. "What don't I understand, Angel? You staying here is already bad enough for your reputation, without us living in the same house. I will not be like my father."

Angel struggled to come up with an explanation she thought Nathan would understand, but she suspected he would only listen to a few words before cutting her off. Her thoughts were clear, but the words remained muddled. In the end, there was only one thing she could tell him. Even though the fire dimly lit the room, the darkness of the storm swirled outside. Safe enough for secrets.

"I'm afraid," she whispered.

WITH WAKEFULNESS CAME REALITY. *Angel no longer found herself on the floor of the saloon as she did every time she dreamed. She was in her own bed and Maria, one of the women who worked at the saloon, was gently smoothing the hair back from her face.*

Angel closed her eyes. Why did it have to be Maria? Maria, who hated her, who jumped at every chance she had to make her squirm, to laugh at her expense.

Maria shifted as she noticed Angel's slight movement. "You're awake," she spoke the obvious.

Angel didn't reply.

"Shame you aren't able to remember more of what happened," Maria said casually. "Are you sure you didn't recognize the man at all?"

Angel, distracted by Maria's tone, spoke uncertainly. "I already told everyone, I don't remember. It was probably someone with a grudge against Tom. That isn't uncommon."

Maria nodded, satisfied, and continued stroking Angel's hair.

"Guess you're not so different from us after all," Maria said softly. Angel opened her eyes again, too emotionally exhausted to protest but unwilling to let the injustice of that statement go unacknowledged. As Angel looked at the other woman, though, she realized there had been no malice in Maria's words, only sadness.

The unexpected feeling in Maria's voice pricked a hole in the hastily laid dam between Angel and the flood of emotions that followed. Unable to stop the words before they left her mouth, or the tear before it trickled down her cheek, Angel whispered, "It hurts."

Her body was stiff, and achy, and felt feverish, and there was a raw hole inside her chest that seemed to be eating itself, growing.

Maria wiped the tear from Angel's cheek and nodded. "I know, sweetie."

"What if he comes back?" Angel asked. "They haven't found him yet. They don't even know who they are looking for."

Maria moved, resting Angel's head carefully against the pillow, and sat so that she could face Angel on the bed. Carefully taking her hand, she looked into Angel's eyes. "We've never been friends. But I'm going to give you some advice, and you can take it or leave it how you want."

Angel waited without interest for the words that were supposed to make her feel better. What would Maria say? That Angel was one of them now? That she was safe? That the girls at the saloon understood? That men were more beasts than human—creatures to be tamed but never trusted? Most of those sentiments Angel had heard repeated by one or another of the saloon girls at some point, although they had never been spoken directly to her.

Maria paused, as though trying to decide how to adequately convey the message she wanted Angel to hear. In the end, Angel thought, Maria must have failed, because the words she spoke rang in Angel's mind like off-key church bells as she drifted back to sleep.

"Don't let anyone know you're afraid, and when the numbness sets in— and it will—don't fight it. Let it take you. Forget what it's like to feel."

"WHAT ARE YOU AFRAID OF?" Nathan asked. All of the previous signs of frustration had been wiped from his face.

Angel shrugged. "Storms, the darkness, being alone." She paused, then added, "That if something happens, there won't be anyone to hear me scream."

Nathan was watching her with a peculiar expression. "That's quite a list. Anything else?"

Her eyes never left his. "That this is all there will ever be—fear and running. Never really being anywhere because I'm always leaving, and nobody caring one way or another."

A half smile rested on Nathan's face. "I asked you to stay."

"You could change your mind."

"I won't."

When Angel didn't respond, Nathan rubbed his hand through his hair. "Guess I'd better go bring that mattress in from the barn."

He sighed as another gust of wind struck the cabin, but he smiled back at Angel when she hesitantly smiled at him. "It'll be okay," he reassured her. "All of it."

Angel watched him as he walked out the door, then turned to gather some blankets to bring to the front room. She laid them out in front of the fire to warm.

When Nathan came back through the door, he looked gratefully at the blankets Angel had laid out, and as they hastily brushed the snow off the mattress, she better understood his gratitude. The cloth was cold to the touch. It wasn't just the kind of cold that would have come from its short journey through the weather. It was the kind of cold that had sunk deep into the mattress, the kind that radiated from the inside out.

As Nathan finished moving the mattress to a corner of the room, he nodded toward the blankets and the fire. "Thank you, Angel."

Angel felt her cheeks flush, and she was glad she could hide behind the warmth of the fire. The strange lightness she had felt when Nathan asked her to stay had returned.

Never before had she thought of a simple thank-you as a compliment. *Thank you*—the words rolled off one's tongue so casually, without thought, more habit than anything else. But Nathan had spoken so sincerely. It was hard not to take the words, "Thank you," for what she thought, in their purest form, they must have originally been meant to be. An expression of appreciation and of approval. An acknowledgement of usefulness and of rightness. A mutual sharing of joy, small or great. *Is it possible to have a small joy?* she wondered then. *Aren't all joys great?*

She walked toward her room, raising her hand to the side of her face and pretending to brush a stray strand of hair back to hide the beginnings of a smile. Before she opened the door, and when she had the smile safely under control, she turned and paused.

"Nathan?" she asked. As he looked up, she said, "Thank you."

"For what?" he asked.

"For everything. For being you."

Nathan grinned, and this time Angel was less successful at hiding the half smile that crept onto her face. She quickly closed the door behind her and, in the darkness, smiled at the soft glow of firelight shining under the door. And still, the strange lightness remained.

7

Every mistake I've ever made has haunted me—ruined me—and made my brother. I gave him his life, his woman. He wouldn't have had any of those things if it hadn't of been for me.

⌇

THE WIND HOWLED through the night. With every gust, the cabin creaked, both resisting the outside forces and settling into them. Every unfamiliar noise startled Angel awake, and she breathed shallowly, quietly, listening for any sounds beneath the noise of the storm before falling back into her restless sleep.

The next morning, Angel groggily opened her eyes, vaguely aware that something had awakened her but unsure what that something might be. She listened for a few moments before it struck her. There were no howling winds, no creaking cabin, no brittle, skeletal branches cracking and snapping—only silence.

Angel reluctantly sat up. The air outside of the covers was freezing, and the touch of the cold wood floor against her bare feet sent goosebumps up her spine. Shivering, she wrapped a blanket around herself and padded barefoot into the main room.

Nathan was already up. The fire was blazing cheerily, and the main room was significantly warmer than the room Angel had slept in. She sighed gratefully as she stepped onto the warm floorboards.

The room smelled wonderful—of pancakes and fresh milk and bacon—and Angel suddenly realized how hungry she was. She hadn't been able to bring herself to eat much the night before, and now she sat down at the table and put her head between her hands, slightly queasy from going so long without food.

"Are you feeling well?" Nathan asked anxiously.

"I'm fine," Angel reassured him. "I'll be fine after I eat." She took a bite of pancake and nibbled on a piece of bacon. "This is good," she said, surprised.

Nathan shrugged, turning another pancake. "No one else was ever gonna cook around here, so I learned. And if I was going to be cooking, I figured I might as well make something worth eating."

"How bad is it out there?" Angel asked.

Nathan shrugged. "The storm's cleared up, but there's at least a foot of snow out there, and the wind blew it into some pretty good drifts. I think the worst of it's over, but it might be a while before we can get out and into town."

Which meant there would be no taking the train out of town.

Angel rose to her feet and walked to the door. Opening it, Angel was faced with a new, glittering world. A pristine blanket of snow covered everything, rising and falling gracefully with lines of the shrubbery and trees beneath. The air was icy and still—Angel's breath rose in shimmering clouds around her as rays of light from the emerging sun danced across the landscape.

"That's something to see," Nathan breathed from beside Angel. He had come to stand beside her, almost without her noticing. Angel nodded without speaking.

"I'm sorry we're snowed in," Nathan said.

Angel gazed out across the blinding landscape. She knew that sooner or later she and Nathan would have to leave the cabin. Sooner or later she would have to go to town. Sooner or later the rumors—

and truths—that had been chasing her would find her and catch her, even here.

But today was not that day.

Today, again, she would pretend.

MILKING BOSSY, the cow, was one task Nathan had decided Angel would safely be able to handle. Despite her initial trepidation, Nathan turned out to be right. Angel soon found taking care of the milk cow to be a relaxing, if somewhat methodical, chore, although she had raised an eyebrow when Nathan first told her the milk cow's name.

"Bossy?" she had asked, looking at the cow skeptically. The cow had seemed to shrug at her, as though to say she could think of no reason to be named such, and then taken a mouthful of hay.

"Yep," Nathan had responded, unconcerned. "Just keep an eye on her—sometimes when she's switching her tail, it'll catch the milk bucket."

Angel had sat hesitantly on the milking stool and, with Nathan's guidance, soon had managed a few weak streams of milk. It had been nothing like the frothy hiss that so rhythmically filled the metal pail when Nathan had demonstrated her new chore, but Angel had nonetheless felt a surprising sense of satisfaction.

"Don't worry," Nathan had told her. "You'll get the hang of it quick enough."

When Nathan had walked out of earshot, she had glanced up at Bossy, who'd turned to look at her.

"Bossy, huh," Angel spoke. "You look more like a Bluebell to me."

The milk cow had stopped twitching her tail. Angel smiled. Bluebell it was.

Now, Angel was used to their morning rhythm. She milked the cow while Nathan worked in the background, finishing the rest of the barn chores. The barn cat waited patiently for her share of the milk, and the chickens fussed.

Nathan walked up and laid his free hand against the milk cow's back; the other held a pitchfork. "Hey, Bossy girl."

Bluebell, who had been chewing her cud, turned her head toward Nathan and coughed, covering him with a spray of moisture. He grimaced as he wiped a hand on his pants.

"She likes the name Bluebell better," Angel told him without looking up from the milk pail. Bluebell turned her head to look at Angel, then mooed a soft rumble as though she were comforting a calf, and Angel rubbed the milk cow's side affectionately.

"Bluebell, huh?" Nathan asked. "I think she just likes you better."

"Probably because I don't call her bossy."

Nathan chuckled and leaned against the pitchfork. "Maybe so."

NATHAN HAD KNOWN the barn cat was due to have a litter of kittens for several weeks, so when five multicolored balls of fur suddenly appeared in the barn one day, he was not surprised. What did surprise him was how quickly Angel became attached to each of the kittens. She loved watching them play or sitting with them in her lap while she stroked their fur and they purred.

Nathan knew that, practically, he couldn't keep all of the cats around, and if Angel hadn't been there, he would likely have followed convention and simply drowned the kittens in the creek. But as he sat beside Angel and scratched the ears of the lone kitten—a white one with black on his ears and paws—that had chosen to sit with Nathan, he couldn't bring himself to follow through on that idea. He knew that if he did, Angel would never forgive him, and as much as he hated to admit it, Nathan was beginning to grow fond of the tiny kittens as well.

Then, one day, the kittens disappeared, and Nathan found the mother cat nursing a nasty gash on the side of her face. Angel spent hours searching for the kittens before finally giving up. Nathan never told Angel about the raccoon he had chased from the barn the evening before, and Angel never mentioned the kittens again. But sometimes, Nathan knew that that when Angel thought he wasn't looking, she spent a few extra moments in the loft or glancing into the kittens' favorite hiding places to make sure they really weren't there.

NATHAN'S favorite time was the evenings, when the chores for the day were done and he and Angel would sit, sometimes talking, sometimes relaxing in easy silence. Often, Angel would sit close to the fire and use the light from its flames to read aloud from Jules Verne's *Journey to the Center of the Earth*, which she told Nathan her parents had given her before the steamboat accident—something to remember France by, they had said.

The animation in Angel's voice when she was reading made Nathan smile. He had no way of knowing how many times Angel had read the book, but if he had to guess, judging by the degree of wear on the cover and the way Angel sometimes continued to speak the words of the book even when she had looked away from the pages to see Nathan's reaction to a particularly exciting passage, he thought it must have been many, many times.

While Angel was reading, Nathan would whittle, shaping small pieces of wood into tiny animals. Angel was always delighted by his carvings and had taken to lining them up on the mantle above the fireplace.

And then sometimes, later in the evening when the fire was dying down, Nathan and Angel would sit, back to back with the heavy wooden door between them, and talk. It seemed so natural in the dark for their conversations to happen this way that it was only in the mornings that Nathan gave their arrangement a second thought. Even then, he only allowed the thought a moment's presence before sloughing it off. If he allowed the thought to remain too long, Nathan was reminded of the strangeness of his and Angel's arrangement, and he didn't want to remember.

8

I've hated my brother for almost as long as I can remember. I've hated
him for living his life, and for stealing mine.

～

ANGEL WOKE to the sound of horse hooves on the packed earth in
front of the cabin and the jingling of harnesses. Nearly two weeks
had passed since the snowstorm, and she had thought she was
becoming used to the sounds of daily life here. This sound was less
familiar.

When Angel walked outside, she saw Nathan hitching the horses
to the wagon. She squinted up at the bright blue sky as the sun
glinted off the still present but slowly shrinking patches of snow.

"Where are you going?" she asked as she drew nearer.

"The road in is better shape, and you've settled in a bit more."
Nathan nodded as he tightened a strap. "Thought I'd head into
town."

Into town. The words halted Angel's footsteps and made her
breath catch in her chest. She and Nathan had been so isolated since
the snowstorm that Angel had almost forgotten there was a world

outside the farm. She wasn't sure she was ready to remember, to trade the security of their tiny world for whatever awaited them outside of it.

"What are you going to do there?" Angel asked, forcing herself to speak normally.

Nathan paused, checking the strap, then spoke as he rose. "Thought I'd go to church. Maybe find out about the train schedule."

"You're going to church?" Angel asked, ignoring Nathan's comment about the train for the time being. "Why?"

Nathan shrugged, glancing at her. "When my father was still around, it was one of two places I knew he would never go. And it was the only place he never tried to stop me from going."

Angel couldn't tell if Nathan was serious. It seemed a strange idea that he might joke about his father letting him go to church. However, of all the places to which she could imagine Nathan's father encouraging attendance, church was not even a hastily scribbled afterthought following a long list of establishments of questionable nature.

Nathan chuckled at Angel's confusion and smiled sarcastically as he said, "Seems like people were more concerned about the salvation of my soul than my physical well-being. It was one thing for my father to take after me with his belt—that was his business. But for him to deny a willing soul the chance to hear the good word? Well, that would have been something else."

He paused, then shrugged. "I used to go to get away from him for a while. Now it's something of a habit, I suppose. Do you want to come?"

Angel hesitated. If Carl and Valentine had done their jobs well, everyone would already have heard that Nathan had been seen in the company of a strange girl. It would come as no surprise to anyone when she and Nathan arrived—together—in town. The only difference Angel expected her appearance would make is that it would replace the townspeople's vague speculation with a clear target. Admittedly, that was not a prospect she looked forward to.

On the other hand, Angel was not eager to remain at the cabin by herself. As terrified as she was at the idea of venturing out from the sanctuary she and Nathan had created for themselves over the last couple weeks, the thought of remaining alone at the cabin scared her even more.

In the end, Angel climbed onto the wagon seat beside Nathan. Nathan clucked his tongue to the horses, and they pulled forward.

"Where was the second place your father wouldn't go?" Angel asked.

Nathan glanced at her with a raised eyebrow. "The graveyard."

"Your father won't go into graveyards?" Angel asked.

Nathan shook his head. "Not all graveyards, I think. Just the one here in town. My mother is buried there." He paused, then added, "Maybe he's afraid of her ghost."

"Why would he be afraid of her ghost?" Angel asked.

"I don't know. I don't remember much about her."

Nathan's hands tightened on the reins, and Angel knew there was something more that Nathan wasn't saying, but she changed the subject.

"What is it going to be like?"

Nathan looked confused at the sudden shift in the conversation. "What will what be like?"

"Church. The people. What will they be like?"

Nathan didn't answer right away. Even though she wasn't surprised by his response, Angel felt the tension begin to creep back into her body.

"Some of them might not be too welcoming," he admitted.

"Then why are we going?"

Nathan glanced at her. "I told you why I'm going. You wanted to come with me, so a better question would probably be why you are going."

Angel was silent. She wasn't ready to admit to Nathan how much being alone still scared her, and she wasn't ready to admit to herself that the idea of leaving on the train was beginning to lose its appeal.

When she didn't respond, Nathan said gently, "It will be okay."

As ANGEL STOOD LOOKING at the rows of pews and the people who were slowly filling them, Nathan watched her inquiringly. Angel had paused in the entryway, and she guessed Nathan was wondering what was holding her back.

She sighed, smoothing her hands down the front of her dress anxiously. It was a new dress, made just the month before, but as she stood outside the church building, the fabric felt uncomfortably tight against her skin. Would anyone notice? And if they did, what would they think?

It wasn't what they would say to her face. It was the words they would whisper just barely loud enough for her to hear as she walked by. Their words wouldn't place the dagger—it had been there so long Angel could hardly remember a time it hadn't been buried uncomfortably between her shoulder blades. But they would twist it deeper.

She slowly raised her eyes to meet Nathan's, answering the question he had not asked. "I believe in Christ. I'm just not sure I believe in Christians."

Nathan raised an eyebrow, and Angel wasn't sure whether he looked amused or shocked. She shrugged. At the resigned motion, one corner of Nathan's mouth lifted slightly.

"You'll have to face them sometime. Might as well be here. There's something about being inside a church. If nothing else, it has a . . . tempering influence."

Angel shrugged again, and Nathan nodded, motioning her to walk on. They made their way into the white building and sat down on a smooth wooden pew in the back row. From there, Angel watched the people filter through the doors. Some glanced inquiringly at her before nodding briefly to Nathan and moving on. Others were more appraising, and Angel struggled to keep from fidgeting as an uncomfortable warmth spread across her body.

She was so distracted that it took her several minutes to notice Nathan's silence. When she did notice, she looked curiously at him, only to see his jaw tightened and his eyes fixed on the front of the room. Angel followed his gaze and was startled to find herself in direct eye contact with a woman who looked oddly familiar. The woman's eyes were narrowed, and as Angel watched, she turned and spoke to the man standing beside her.

The man had to bend down slightly to hear her. He was much taller than the woman, and he too looked oddly familiar. As the woman finished speaking, the man glanced at Angel and Nathan, nodding.

The actions of the man and woman seemed to draw the attention of a young woman sitting in the front pew; she turned to search the faces of the people sitting in the rows behind her. When her eyes finally landed on Nathan, she smiled and waved enthusiastically. Nathan's glower disappeared for a moment as he nodded slightly to her—more acknowledgement than he had given the older couple. The older woman laid her hand on the shoulder of the young woman who had waved, and she turned around to once again face the front of the room.

"Who are they?" Angel asked.

"They must have just come into town. When I heard the old preacher and his wife were leaving, I didn't realize Clark and Olivia would be taking their place."

Nathan did not look happy with his realization.

"You are acquainted with them?" Angel asked.

"In a manner of speaking."

"They look familiar," Angel commented. "I wonder if I should recognize them from somewhere?"

"I hope not," Nathan muttered, but when Angel looked at him questioningly, he didn't offer any additional information.

"How do you know them?"

Nathan stared ahead at the front of the room. As Angel glanced again toward the couple holding Nathan's attention, she saw the woman appear to meet Nathan's eyes and give a slight nod. Without acknowledging the woman's gesture, Nathan abruptly turned to Angel and spoke.

"Sisters married brothers. Olivia is my mother's sister," Nathan spoke darkly. "And Clark is my father's brother. Felicity is their daughter."

Now it was Angel's turn to stare, first at Nathan and then at the couple. The odd familiarity suddenly made sense. As she looked back and forth from Nathan to his aunt and uncle, she couldn't keep the astonishment from her voice.

"Why wouldn't they tell you they were coming?" Angel asked.

Nathan shrugged. "I haven't seen or heard from them in years. Why would they?"

THE AIR WAS FILLED with quiet noises—the shifting of the congregation, the squeaking of the pews, the buzzing of a fly in the window behind them. Nathan wondered how he could at once be so focused on the man at the front of the room and yet hear none of the words he was speaking. The man's mouth was moving, but it seemed to move muddily, and both the shapes and sounds of the words were blurred.

Nathan thought his own expression must have carried a scowl, because once, and only once, the man had looked directly at Nathan and seemed to be thrown out of the rhythm of his sermon. He had paused, open-mouthed, before quickly looking down at his notes to regain his place.

Clark and Olivia. His aunt and uncle. The words left a bad taste in Nathan's mouth, and he resisted saying them, even in his mind. If he spoke them, it felt like both an acknowledgement and revival of family ties that had long been dead, and Nathan cared to do neither. Felicity, his cousin, was not so bad, but Nathan guessed whatever the reason for her presence, she wouldn't be staying long. Not much older than Nathan himself, Felicity had always been more independent than her mother and father would have preferred.

Angel sat beside Nathan, furtively shooting him sidelong glances. He felt more than saw the pricks of her curiosity, and he closed his eyes as he rested his forehead against his fists. To anyone who happened to look his way, he might appear to be praying. The thought made Nathan smile with dark amusement. His head was bowed over hands clenched in anger, not prayer. Why had his aunt and uncle come back? They had been gone for so long.

WHEN THE SERMON ENDED, Nathan stood to stretch, and Angel followed suit, grateful for the opportunity to allow motion to dispel some of the tension she felt. Almost immediately, Felicity made her way through the congregation to stand beside Nathan and Angel.

"Felicity," Nathan nodded. Angel watched him closely. He spoke stiffly as he greeted the woman, but without any of the animosity he had held toward his aunt and uncle.

Felicity, on the other hand, had no such inhibitions. "Cousin Nathan," she smiled warmly, "it is good to see you again."

Nathan smiled in response to Felicity's openness. "What brings you all the way out here? Besides the obvious, I mean." Nathan nodded toward the front of the room where Clark and Olivia still remained.

"I accepted a teaching position farther west. Mama and Papa had already decided to come here, so I decided to travel with them. I'll only be staying here for a few days—I'll start teaching next week."

"And how do Clark and Olivia feel about you taking that job?" Nathan asked. Felicity hesitated, and Nathan grinned. "None too happy, I'm guessing?"

Felicity glanced at her parents, then smiled and laughed reluctantly. "No, but they will get used to the idea."

Abruptly changing the subject, Felicity turned toward Angel and said, "Since my cousin seems to have forgotten to introduce us—"

Nathan interrupted in protest, but Felicity ignored him and kept speaking. "We will have to do so ourselves. As you have probably guessed, I am Felicity. Nathan and I are cousins."

Angel smiled. "Yes, you and Nathan look so alike. I should have guessed you were related."

Felicity nodded. "I've heard that often." She laughed lightly. "But I suppose that is to be expected when sisters marry brothers. Mama always says I look a bit of her and a lot of my father, but I don't see it. I think the family resemblance becomes more apparent when you see us all together—not that you would ever want to see that." Here, she made a wide gesture with her arms, and Angel thought Felicity must have meant to include herself and her parents, as well as Nathan and his parents in her imaginary circle.

"But you still haven't told me your name," Felicity gently reminded Angel.

Angel began speaking out of reflex. "My name is Angel. And I'm glad to meet you."

And here, Angel stopped speaking. She could tell from Felicity's expectant expression that she was waiting for an explanation of how Angel knew her cousin. Angel glanced at Nathan, who shrugged.

Felicity watched the uncomfortable exchange, waited a brief moment, and then prodded. "How did you make my cousin's acquaintance?"

Angel opened her mouth, then closed it, trying to find a way to explain to Felicity that she and Nathan had met seven years ago on the front steps of a saloon—an explanation that would surely lead to the fact that she was now staying at Nathan's home—when Nathan's voice interrupted her thoughts.

"She's staying with me."

Eyebrows raised, Felicity turned to Nathan. "That's an . . . interesting arrangement," Felicity said slowly.

Nathan shrugged again. "She needed help."

Felicity considered Angel for a moment. Then her expression softened as she spoke. "Well then, you went to the right person."

Shock drove the ability to speak from Angel's mouth, and before Angel could think of a response to Felicity's statement, Clark and Olivia appeared to stand on either side of their daughter.

"Nathan," Olivia said, nodding to him. He nodded stiffly back. Olivia then turned to Angel. "I believe I have yet to make your acquaintance, dear."

Once again, Angel found herself unsure and her tongue tied. Nathan clearly held Clark and Olivia in contempt. Angel felt as though she had been awkwardly deposited into the middle of an argument she knew nothing about and was now afraid to offend either party, completely unaware what had transpired to bring about the argument in the first place.

Felicity, noticing Angel's discomfort, interjected, "Mama, Papa, this is Angel. She is staying with Nathan. She needed help."

Olivia's eyebrows shot up, and suddenly Angel could clearly see the resemblance between Olivia and Felicity. Clark gritted his teeth and turned to face Nathan, who closed his eyes, rubbed his forehead, and muttered, "Oh, Felicity."

Angel fought the urge to draw closer to Nathan as Clark's expression darkened. Clark pounced on Nathan's words, speaking tersely while keeping his voice low to avoid attracting attention from the remaining members of the congregation as they exited the building. "Did you expect Felicity to keep this from us?"

"No," Nathan growled, "but—"

"This is neither the time nor the place," Clark said, cutting Nathan off. "We will discuss this later."

"Discuss?" Nathan asked quietly.

Clark, appearing not to notice Nathan's tone, continued on unabashed. "Yes, we will discuss the . . . impropriety . . . of your situation later."

"We will be discussing nothing," Nathan said, his voice dangerously low. "You are not my father, and you did nothing to keep me from him when you had the chance. You have no place in my life and no right to discuss it."

Angel looked back and forth between the equally furious Nathan and Clark, the apologetic Felicity, and the flustered Olivia, and found herself suddenly angry at being used as a pawn in their argument. Her presence was not even the catalyst for this fight, she realized. It was the excuse.

"Excuse me," she said quietly, satisfied to note that her voice held no tremor, "but I want no part of this."

The four seemed surprised to hear her voice, as though they had forgotten she was there. Angel continued. "Your nephew offered me aid, and I chose to accept his kindness. Our situation is nothing more and nothing less. It might be improper, but it is not immoral. I would thank you all"—and here she looked pointedly at Nathan—"to leave me from this discussion."

Angel nodded at Felicity. "It was nice to have met you." And, avoiding Nathan's eyes, she walked out the church doors to where the horse and wagon stood waiting.

NATHAN STOOD FROZEN beside his cousin and aunt and uncle until the abrupt sound of the church doors closing shook him, and ignoring the jumbled words that spilled all at once in a tangled mess from the others, he ran after Angel.

He found her, shivering, in the seat of the wagon. "This was a terrible idea."

"Which part?" he asked. "Staying with me, coming to church, speaking to Clark and Olivia, or . . ." He paused, then trying to lighten the mood, he finished, "me being related to my family?"

"All of it," she said miserably. Then Angel paused, apparently realizing how what she had just said must have sounded. She covered her face and buried her head in her lap. "I didn't mean it that way."

Nathan thought he should have been offended, but instead, he couldn't help smiling. "I know."

Angel still refused to look at him. Finally, even as he was aware of a small group of remaining people who stood outside the church, whispering in scandalized tones and watching them carefully—Clark and Olivia stood silently at the front of the group—Nathan reached over to gently tip her chin up until she looked him in the eyes.

"Stand tall, Angel. You didn't—you haven't—done anything wrong."

Nathan saw the words paint themselves across her face. The corner of Angel's mouth lifted briefly, then fell, and she hastily scrubbed a tear from her cheek. Nathan pretended he hadn't seen, instead looking past Angel toward where Clark and Olivia stood. Clark's expression was distant and disapproving. Nathan glanced at Olivia, expecting to see a similar reflection, but was surprised to realize she was not even looking at him. Olivia's expression was thoughtful, her eyebrows pinched, and she had eyes only for Angel.

9

If saving my brother was my first mistake, the drinking was the second.

❧

"Did you mean what you said?" Angel asked, shaking Nathan from his reverie. Their trip home had been mostly silent, with both Angel and Nathan absorbed in their own thoughts.

Nathan sifted through his memory. He couldn't remember much of what he had said since he had first recognized Clark and Olivia at the church, and most of what he could remember wasn't particularly pleasant.

"What I said about what?" he asked

Angel hesitated, slow to repeat the words. "That I haven't done anything wrong."

Nathan glanced at her, surprised by Angel's question and struck by a sudden pang of sadness that she had felt the need to ask it. "Yes, I meant it. Why?"

Angel's voice was small. "You were so angry when you recognized me that first day."

Inwardly, Nathan cringed. He was ashamed of much of what he had said in that conversation, but as much as he hated his own memory of how he had acted, the thought of Angel remembering those moments was worse. Nathan shook his head. He knew why he had acted as he had, but he wasn't sure the reason would make a difference to Angel.

"Yes, you were," Angel argued, interrupting Nathan's thoughts, interpreting the shake of his head as a denial. She continued softly. "You were awful."

Nathan turned toward her. Despite the fact that Angel had just called him awful, he couldn't help admiring her stubborn vulnerability. Besides, he wouldn't deny what Angel had said. Nathan knew he had been unkind.

He wanted to search her face. Angel sometimes spoke with such openness that it caught him off guard, but those times were so few and far between that Nathan had begun to suspect he would find the truth more often in the nuance of her expression than in the words themselves. But at the moment Angel was adamantly focusing her attention somewhere near the twitching ears of the team pulling the wagon.

"I know I was unkind. I'm sorry for that," Nathan said.

Angel glanced at him. "You already said you were sorry."

It was obvious she expected something more. Nathan knew it was the why. And the how. Why he had been so angry, and how that could have changed so quickly. But Nathan didn't want to speak about it, so he asked her a question instead.

"What else do you want me to say?" he asked.

Angel eyed him, then shrugged and shook her head. "Nothing."

That was a lie. Nathan knew it was a lie. But then, he thought, he had known what she wanted from him but had asked anyway, hoping for the answer she had obligingly given—nothing—so his question had not been wholly truthful either.

"I spoke with the telegraph operator today. The train should be in early next week," Nathan said, changing the subject. Angel nodded, acknowledging his words but saying nothing.

The remainder of their trip home passed in silence.

As did the afternoon.

And the evening.

After Nathan had climbed into his bed, he lay with his hands behind his head, staring past the ceiling. A small noise interrupted his thoughts—the lifting of a door latch and then a soft voice.

"Nathan?"

"Yeah?"

"Please tell me why."

Nathan groaned internally. This was not a conversation he wanted to have—the thought of trying to explain the thoughts that had been racing through his mind all day made him cringe—but he forced himself to roll out of bed and walk toward Angel's room. As he crossed the room, he heard the soft *thud-click* of a door shutting and a metal latch falling back into place. It was the sound of late-night conversations through solid doors, a familiar sound. He relaxed.

Still, the words were so slow in coming that he thought Angel must be wondering if he was going to speak at all. Finally, ignoring the sour feeling in his stomach and the pounding heart in his chest, he took a long, deep breath and exhaled slowly, steadying himself before he began speaking.

"It's not normal to care so much about someone you've only known for not even a day—I know it's not. But you were my lifeline. Up until that day there were so many voices—some real, some inside my own head—telling me my life was a mistake, and that's all my life would ever be. And then I met you. You were everything my father was not. When I was with you, everything didn't hurt. Part of me thought you really were an angel. I swear I know how crazy that sounds, but when I met you, for the first time I believed that someday my life could be different than what it was.

"Every day afterward I lived and breathed that memory. Then, when I stopped in town and talked to the storekeeper that day I met you on the road and he told me . . ."

Nathan's voice trailed off, and Angel spoke flatly, picking up where he had left off. "Man to man."

The words sounded even worse when Angel said it out loud than they had inside his own head, and Nathan cringed, but continued speaking. "Up to that point, in my mind you were this real-life angel who hadn't been hurt by anyone or anything, who could fix all the brokenness around them. Even after I stopped needing to believe that was true, I still wanted it to be."

"And then the angel you had imagined died in the same moment you recognized me."

Nathan nodded, painfully, even though he knew Angel couldn't see him. "I blamed you for that. I know I was cruel—the worst part is that I meant to be—but I was wrong and I'm sorry.

"After you told me what happened, and I realized it wasn't your fault . . . I don't know. It was easy to justify saying what I said before I knew the truth about what had happened. After you told me, all I could think was how awful I'd been. I'm sorry."

There was a long moment of silence, and then Angel spoke. "You'll never think of me the same as you used to, will you?"

It was more of a statement than a question, begging confirmation rather than an answer, but Nathan thought carefully before he responded.

"Nah," he said, "but if I did think of you the same as I always had, it would be because we'd never met again. Real people change, Angel, and I'm glad you're real. I'm glad you're real, and I'm glad you're here."

When Angel was silent, Nathan added, "I know that all sounds crazy."

"Maybe," Angel said, and he could hear a slight smile in her voice, "but it sounds nice too."

They sat in silence for a moment, and then Angel asked, "Your aunt and uncle—Clark and Olivia? Are they really so bad?"

"They knew what my father was, and they left me with him," Nathan answered simply, "but if you want to get to know them, I'm sure you'll have your chance. It looks like they're going to be around for a while."

"It's odd to think your father's brother is a preacher."

Nathan snorted his agreement. "Yes, it is."

"Is Clark like your father?"

"Maybe in some ways. I think Clark has a temper, but he's better at controlling it than my father was. My father never had anything good to say about Clark, but I guess he's never really had much good to say about anybody. As far as I know, Clark hated my father, and hates me too, because I'm my father's son."

Angel closed her eyes against the now-familiar twinge in her chest and rested the back of her head against the door. It wasn't right. She had no right. No right to feel anything toward Nathan other than the debt of gratitude she owed him for his kindness. No right to hope for anything more.

She was pregnant with another man's child. She hadn't started to show yet, but she knew she would soon. And then what?

The daydreams of childhood were not for someone like her, and when she caught her mind wandering down that path, she forced herself to answer the question. *And what then, Angel?* she asked herself harshly. Even if he could possibly care for you beyond the simple kindness he's shown you, could you ask him to be a father to your fatherless child?

The answer was always no.

10

I once heard it said that a moral was something a man would stand by, no matter what. I guess I don't have any morals—not once the whiskey's inside of me.

THE NEXT MORNING, Angel woke to the sound of arguing.

"How long has she been here?"

"A couple weeks," Nathan's voice answered.

"Nathan." This time it was a female voice that spoke, softly, more encouragingly. "Why is she really here?"

Nathan's raised voice again came through the door. "It's not your place to care one way or another. You haven't been in my life for years, and certainly not during any part of it when you would have been of some use. None of this concerns you."

Angel cracked the door open just in time to see Clark step toward Nathan.

Nathan's entire body was rigid, stony. Then, his head tilted slightly as one eyebrow rose. The words were not spoken, but they screamed through the air. *Are you sure you want to do that?*

Clark looked at his hand, clenching the collar of Nathan's shirt. He looked up at Nathan, who stared evenly at him.

"Clark," Olivia said softly. Clark released his grip on Nathan's collar, stepping back and shaking himself as though only just realizing what he had been doing. He seemed to look at Olivia for direction, stunned.

"Clark," Olivia repeated. "Nathan is not his father."

"I—I'm sorry," Clark stammered to Nathan. He closed his eyes, shaking himself again, then said more firmly, "I'm sorry, Nathan. Your father and I have not been on good terms for quite some time, you should know—"

"Nobody is on good terms with my father," Nathan interrupted him.

"Yes, well," Clark continued stiffly. "I apologize for taking out my feelings toward your father on you."

"Everybody does."

The three stood in uncomfortable silence. Finally, Olivia said, "Nathan, why is Angel here?"

"Felicity already told you—she needed help," Nathan answered.

Angel cleared her throat, and almost as one, they turned to look at her. Nathan looked relieved to see her, with traces of the frustration that had been directed at Clark still evident on his face. Olivia's face held a rather unnerving expression of concern. Clark merely looked pained.

"Nathan was just telling us that you've been staying here the last few weeks," Olivia finally said, breaking the silence.

Unsure of how much information to offer, Angel said uncomfortably, "Just the last two weeks." Looking at Nathan, she added, "Nathan was staying in the barn, but then it got so cold. He brought his mattress in and he's been staying inside since then."

Even as Angel spoke, she could feel the awkwardness of her words. She glanced from Nathan to Clark to Olivia. Nathan appeared mildly amused by her explanation. She had no idea how to interpret Clark's expression. And Olivia. Olivia was watching her thoughtfully, with eyes that seemed to hold a greater depth of understanding than Angel thought her own abbreviated explanation could have elicited.

"How long are you and Olivia planning on being here?" Nathan asked Clark, drawing his aunt and uncle's attention away from Angel, much to her relief. "Is this appointment temporary, or will you be here longer?"

"Well," said Clark, glancing at Olivia, "we thought we'd try it out and see how it goes. We will be here at least through the first part of spring."

Nathan scowled and opened his mouth, but Olivia interjected quickly, "Will we be seeing you both next Sunday, perhaps at church and then for supper afterward?"

Nathan and Clark both froze. It was obvious that neither had anticipated Olivia's offer. Angel eyed both of them, but when neither spoke, she turned to Olivia.

"That is very kind. Thank you for your offer. We will see you on Sunday."

Where Nathan and Clark had been focused on Olivia, as one they redirected their attention toward Angel. She tried to ignore them, focusing instead on Olivia's warm smile. Olivia glanced at Nathan and Clark, then spoke briskly. "Well, I think we've kept you long enough. We'll let you get back to your day."

As they walked out the door, Clark turned and laid a hand on Nathan's shoulder. Nathan's body tensed, but Clark met his eyes.

"I am truly sorry for my actions earlier, Nathan. You have so much of your father's look that I sometimes forget you don't necessarily have his heart."

The qualifying word did not escape Nathan's notice, and he tried to shake off Clark's hand. "Necessarily."

Clark's grip tightened on Nathan's shoulder. "Yes, necessarily. I hope for your sake, and hers"—he nodded toward Angel—"that you don't. You would be better off with as little of your father as possible."

"This from someone who left me with him for—how long has it been, Clark?" The cold glint in Nathan's eyes told Angel he knew exactly how long it had been. "The last time I saw the both of you was at my mother's funeral."

Clark stiffened and drew back from Nathan. "It's not that simple. There were things that you knew—you still know—nothing about. We were lucky to even come to your mother's funeral. I said it was a foolish risk, but Olivia insisted—"

"A foolish risk?" Nathan's voice grated, rising as he spoke. "Is that what attending my mother's funeral was to you—a foolish risk?

"Perhaps that was a poor choice of words," Clark said hotly, "but it was a risk. You don't know—"

"I don't know?" Nathan cut him off again, but this time his voice was barely audible. Dangerously quiet. "Tell me what exactly I don't know about my father. That he's a drunk? That he's dangerous? That he beat me—his own son—within an inch of my life, and probably killed my mother?"

Clark looked at Nathan with something close to sympathy, and this time when he spoke, the words were quiet and firm, almost gentle. "There are things even you don't know about your father, Nathan."

Stunned, Nathan stepped back from Clark, and disbelief and fury flashed over his face. Clark turned to Olivia, already perched on the wagon seat and silently watching their exchange. "We should go."

He nodded at Angel and Nathan, then climbed into the wagon. He hesitated briefly before he said, "I do hope we'll still see you on Sunday," then he clucked his tongue at the horses, and Clark and Olivia pulled forward. Olivia took Clark's hand in hers, then turned to nod her goodbyes. Angel waved from inside the cabin door. Clark did not look back.

Angel didn't dare speak to Nathan. His eyes were flashing as he stalked past the door, heading toward the barn. After a few minutes had passed, she followed his path out the cabin door and stood on the porch. She could see him pitching hay down from the loft to the animals below, and as she watched the vigor with which he was attacking his task, Angel better understood how he had managed to keep the property in such immaculate condition by himself. If his current behavior was any indication, Nathan was in the habit of taking out his anger on the farm chores, and Angel imagined his father had provided an ample source of frustration.

She did not see Nathan the rest of the morning. Or afternoon.

Angel was already in her room and had turned down the covers of the bed when a creak of the cabin door and footsteps on the wood floor announced Nathan's return. The footsteps paused, then grew subtly louder. The soft rap of knuckles on hardwood came slowly, hesitantly.

"Yes?" Angel asked.

"I wanted to apologize for earlier," Nathan said. "I wish you hadn't have had to see that."

When Angel didn't speak, Nathan continued. "Clark and I have our own differences with my father. You'd think that would be enough to help us get along—give us something in common, anyway. Funny how the one thing we have in common is the one thing we dislike the most about each other. My father."

Angel could almost see him shaking his head on the other side of the door.

"Anyway, I just wanted to tell you I'm sorry."

Again, Nathan paused, waiting for Angel to speak. She hesitated, uncertain whether he was seeking reassurance or condemnation, unsure whether he would accept the former and unwilling to give the latter. She chose middle ground and offered neither.

"Please don't dwell on this, Nathan."

"I want you to feel comfortable here," Nathan protested. "I don't want you to think—"

"I am comfortable here," Angel said firmly, cutting him off. "I'm not worried about Clark and Olivia, and I don't think less of you."

Nathan digested her words, then softly said, "Thank you."

They sat quietly until a giggle broke the silence.

"What?" Nathan asked.

"You should have seen your face when Olivia invited us for

dinner. You and Clark both." Angel laughed. "You both looked so terrified."

"Olivia has that effect," Nathan muttered.

Usually Angel felt it was she who drew out these late-night conversations, but this time it was Nathan who lingered at the door. So, Angel asked the question that had been on her mind since Clark and Olivia had left that morning.

"Nathan, what happened to your mother?"

Nathan was silent for a long moment before he finally answered, "Nobody really knows."

"Nobody knows? But when you were talking to Clark, you said—"

"I know, I said my father probably killed my mother. And he probably did. But I guess nobody knows for sure except for him."

"What do you think?" Angel prompted.

"I think if you listen between the lines of the gossip that goes around town, you'll eventually hear enough partial truths to guess what really happened."

Angel closed her eyes and leaned her head back against the door. "And what exactly was the talk that went around town?"

Nathan exhaled slowly. "Oh, that she was always throwing herself at other men, that she was never happy with my father, and that she had probably been unfaithful to him. That he must have found out and killed her for it. They found her at the bottom of a cliff down by the river. It was a strange spot to have fallen. They never found any real evidence that my father had anything to do with it though."

Angel was beginning to understand that the more brusquely Nathan spoke, the more the words he was saying bothered him.

"And you think that's why he wouldn't go to the graveyard—he was afraid of seeing your mother's ghost because he killed her?"

"Seems like a good reason to me."

Angel pondered this thought, then shuddered. "That's horrible."

"Yeah," Nathan agreed.

"Do you really think that your mother would have done all those things?" Angel asked.

"I don't know what to believe." Nathan sounded tired on the other side of the door. "I know what my father was like, and it's hard to believe any decent woman would have wanted to marry him."

"Olivia would have known her better than anyone. Maybe you should ask her about your mother."

"I am not talking to Olivia." Nathan's tone was carefully even.

"Why not?" Angel asked. "Clark and Olivia are the best chance you have at any sort of real answer."

"I don't want answers from them," Nathan insisted stubbornly.

"Even if they are the only ones who might have the answers you are looking for?"

"They left me with my father," Nathan said slowly, enunciating each word. That one fact, in Nathan's mind—and it was apparent he thought Angel should agree—was clearly more than enough reason for him to want nothing to do with his aunt and uncle, but he added, "Besides, Clark didn't seem any too eager to offer any answers while he was here."

"But they're your family," Angel said softly.

"So is my father"—Nathan laughed without humor—"and I would be glad if I never saw him again."

"You seem to get on well with Felicity."

"Felicity is not like Clark and Olivia."

Angel was silent. She could feel Nathan's frustration radiating from the opposite side of the door. The lull in conversation lasted so long Angel was nearly ready to stand and crawl beneath the warm covers of her bed when Nathan spoke. "Do you mind if I ask you something, Angel?"

"I suppose not," she answered hesitantly.

"It's just, you never really talk about your life before you came here, even when you were still living with your uncle. I don't blame you for not talking about it much, but if you don't mind, sometime I'd like to hear more about it—what it was like growing up at the saloon."

Angel supposed she should have expected Nathan to ask sooner or later, but the question still caught her off guard. "Why?"

Nathan shrugged. "Almost everything I know about you is from seven years ago, what you told me when we were sitting out in front of the saloon. I guess I'd like to know some of what happened in between."

Exhaling a long breath of air, Angel leaned the back of her head against the door. Nathan was right. She hadn't spoken of the saloon often, primarily because she preferred not to think of the saloon often.

Nathan spoke quickly. "It's fine if you don't want—"

Angel interrupted him. "No. I don't mind telling you. Is there anything in particular you'd like to know?"

Nathan shook his head. "No, I guess not."

Angel thought for a moment, sifting through and discarding memories. "I did a lot of laundry while I was there. I cleaned. I learned a lot about medicine—that was the part I enjoyed most.

"My father was a doctor before he died, and when I was very young, the doctor in town would sometimes show me what he was doing when he worked on some of the women at the saloon. He was the one who showed me how to make the salve I put on your back when you and I were children—he told me he learned it from a Sioux medicine man."

Here Angel stopped speaking, but Nathan remained silent, waiting for something more. Angel shook her head at herself. Nathan knew about her nightmares, her attack, her uncle's murder. He knew about the death of her parents and her history at the saloon. He knew so much about her life, and yet it was still hard for her to answer his question the way she knew he wanted, instead giving him impersonal details of her day-to-day life. She took a deep breath and spoke the first memory that came to mind.

"When I was younger, right after I had moved there to stay with my uncle, the girls at the saloon fairly fawned over me. They loved dressing me up and doing my hair and makeup. I think they thought of me almost as a life-sized doll. Tom ignored it for the most part.

"Then when I was twelve, things started changing. I remember one night the girls dressed me up. I thought I looked beautiful. They walked me down the stairs to show me off, and every man in the saloon got quiet. Most of them were looking at Tom. Then one of the men in the saloon whistled and Tom lost it. He threw that man out of the saloon, yelling at him to never set foot in his establishment again. He was so furious, he yelled at all the girls, asked them what they were thinking, told them they had no right, said they were never to do anything like that again. After that, nothing was the same. I think the girls hated me because Tom had made me different. They started talking about how I was giving myself airs and thought I was better than them ..."

Angel's voice trailed off. She was suddenly acutely aware of the deep silence on the other side of the door. Why had she chosen that memory?

Nathan seemed stunned and was silent for a long while. Finally, he said, "You said you stayed at the saloon all those years because you didn't have anywhere else to go. What about now? Are you staying here because you want to, or because you don't have any other options?"

Both the earnestness of Angel's reply, and the quickness with which it came, surprised her. "I've been more glad to stay than you will probably ever know."

From the other side of the door, Nathan's voice was so warm Angel could almost see the smile on his face as he spoke. "For what it's worth, I'm glad you're here."

Again, Angel waited for Nathan to speak, but when he didn't, she followed her wandering thoughts, and then laughed into the silence.

"What are you laughing about?" Nathan asked.

"Clark reminds me of someone I used to see around the saloon."

"Clark wouldn't let himself be caught dead in a place like that," Nathan protested.

"Probably not," Angel agreed. "But all the same, he reminds me of someone there."

"And what sort of man was he—the one Clark reminds you of?"

Angel shrugged. "The kind that falls in love with one of the girls and is lucky enough to actually have it all work out through sheer, stubborn belief in the impossible."

"So in this story, that would make Olivia a saloon girl?" Nathan sounded amused at the idea, and Angel snorted inelegantly.

"You can tease me all you want, but when I was a girl, I used to sit on the stairs in the saloon and watch the men and women dancing and drinking, talking on the floor below. You learn people real fast that way."

"Tell me about some of the other people."

Angel thought. "There were some men who would come in and be belligerent from the start. They always caused trouble, but we knew they would, so it wasn't so bad—they were predictable.

"There were others who would come in real smooth, smiling, not doing anything wrong but making everyone uneasy for some reason no one could explain. They'd do and say all the right things until something didn't go their way, and then in an instant they'd go from smooth talking to making threats you knew wouldn't wear off with the alcohol. But the thing is, you never knew what would set them off.

"The belligerent ones weren't so bad. They mostly only broke glass or furniture. The smooth ones liked to break people."

"Do you remember my father at all?" Nathan asked.

Angel hesitated, then reluctantly said, "Yes."

"What type was he?"

Angel hesitated still longer before answering, "Mean."

There was a long silence, and then Nathan spoke. "And me—if I were a person at your saloon, what type would I be?"

Angel smiled. "You're the kind that sits outside and talks to a ten-year-old girl rather than going inside."

Angel could hear a slight smile in his voice as he replied, but his words were serious. "Maybe. But Clark wouldn't go in either, and you still said he was a type. What type do you think I would be?"

Angel swallowed before she answered. She refused to let sadness, or wistfulness, or hopefulness, or any other -ness color her words. "You're the type who comes in for a drink almost every day at the exact same time. You don't laugh or swap stories with the other men.

You don't gamble. And you're completely oblivious to the fact that one of the girls is in love with you, even though she tries to talk to you every day you come in."

"That's a type?" Nathan asked incredulously. "What sort of man doesn't realize a girl's in love with him when they talk every day?"

"Yes, Nathan, that's a type. And you would be surprised."

11

I forced the woman who would become my brother's wife. It wasn't her fault. I was angry with my brother—jealous. As soon as I sobered up enough to realize what I'd done, I went straight back to the saloon to drown my conscience. And it worked, until I sobered up again. After that, the drinking became more than just my vice. It became my life.

THE FOLLOWING Sunday morning found Nathan and Angel, once again, on their way to church. This time, however, it was Nathan who fidgeted on the way to town, jiggling his left leg so rapidly that the wagon seat shook more from his restless movement than from that of its wheels jolting over the frozen, uneven road. Nathan did not want to be in the same room as Clark and Olivia, he did not want to be preached to by Clark, and he certainly did not want to eat Sunday dinner with them.

As they walked through the church doors together for the second time, Nathan thought he must be feeling some of the same anxiety Angel had felt that first Sunday. He was more aware of the scrutiny of those around them, and as Clark moved, stepping forward to speak,

Nathan hunched down in his seat, afraid of what Clark's message would be.

Clark took his place at the front of the room, and then, looking in Nathan's direction, began to speak. "Judge not, that ye be not judged."

Nathan jerked his head up with a jolt and scowled at Clark, who continued speaking, unfazed. Nathan couldn't tell whether Clark's words had been intended to be an apology or a condemnation. All he knew for sure was that those opening words had been directed at him and Angel, and he wasn't inclined to give Clark's motivations the benefit of the doubt.

He found himself wishing Clark would have hit him when he and Olivia had visited the cabin those few days ago. Then Nathan could have done what he'd wanted to do for some time—although most of the time he wouldn't admit it to himself—and split his knuckles against Clark's face. He wouldn't have had to feel guilty about fighting Clark. They were evenly matched, and he figured Clark would have been about as glad as Nathan himself to finally have it out.

The sad thing, Nathan thought, was that if he and Clark were ever to fight, they might be hitting each other, but they would be throwing fists at his father. Nathan shook his head in disgust, looking back up at Clark, who met his eyes and nodded just barely. Nathan raised two fingers in mock salute, and Clark's face darkened. Still holding his uncle's eyes, Nathan smiled. Clark held Nathan's gaze long enough to show that he recognized the challenge, then broke eye contact. Not once did Clark falter in his speaking.

AFTER THE SERVICE WAS OVER, Nathan and Angel made their way to Clark and Olivia's home—Angel with far less reluctance than Nathan. Nathan eyed Angel as they came to the white fence that bordered his aunt and uncle's house, almost envying her. She seemed relaxed, and even though Nathan suspected Angel was maintaining her distance from his relatives for his sake, he knew she was looking forward to seeing Olivia.

As they approached the front door, Nathan raised his hand to the door to knock, then paused and exhaled heavily in resignation. Angel lightly touched his arm, and when he turned to look at her questioningly, she smiled encouragingly.

Nathan had scarcely knocked on the door once before Olivia answered the door with a cheerful and welcoming smile.

She said, "I'm so glad to see you both," and ushered them into the house. Constantly moving about the kitchen, Olivia talked while she checked a temperature here, set a place there.

"Supper is still a few minutes out, but we should be eating soon. Please make yourselves at home. Angel, would you please fetch that serving platter from the shelf over there? Nathan, Clark is in the back room. You might want to visit with him and let him know supper will be ready soon."

Olivia was still chatting when Nathan walked out of the room. He slowly walked down the hall until he came to a door that was cracked open. It creaked as Nathan pulled it open further, and Clark turned to face him, expressionless. Clark watched Nathan in silence until Nathan finally spoke, his voice low and flat. "Oliva asked me to tell you supper's almost ready."

Without waiting, Nathan turned to walk back to the kitchen. He heard Clark stand behind him and then begin to speak. "Nathan—"

But Clark's words were cut off by the sound of porcelain shattering and the heavy thud of a body falling to the floor.

"Clark," Olivia's sharp voice called, "come now."

To his credit, Nathan thought, Clark almost moved faster in that moment than Nathan himself. They arrived at the kitchen together, both breathless with fear of what they might see. Olivia was kneeling frantically beside Angel, shards of what must have been the serving platter strewn across the floor.

ANGEL WOKE WITH CLARK, Olivia, and Nathan kneeling anxiously beside her. Olivia's hand rested on Angel's forehead, and Nathan and

Clark were quietly arguing about whether or not one of them should fetch the doctor. As they saw that she was awake, Clark and Nathan silenced their bickering, and Olivia asked, "How are you feeling, dear? Can I get you something to drink, something to eat?"

Angel slowly raised herself onto her elbows and looked around. The porcelain platter lay scattered across the floor in pieces—a sight that felt uncomfortably familiar, especially when Nathan shifted, accidentally crushing a piece of porcelain beneath his foot. Suppressing the urge to hug her knees to her chest, Angel closed her eyes against the memory of another day she had woken on the floor, disoriented and surrounded by shattered glass. As she pushed the memory away, embarrassment flooded over her.

"I'm so sorry," she whispered. "I didn't mean to break your plate."

Horrified, she realized tears were welling in her eyes, and she covered her face with her hands.

Immediately, Olivia took Angel's hands in her own. "Please don't worry about that, dear." She waved a hand. "It wasn't anything important anyway."

Nathan raised an eyebrow, an expression Olivia diligently ignored as she asked again, "Would you like something to eat?"

The thought of the stew cooking on the stove made Angel's stomach cringe, but she managed a weak smile. "I feel silly. I was so afraid we would be late this morning that I forgot to eat breakfast before we left. I'd just like to lie down for a while, if that is all right, and then I will eat something and should be fine."

Olivia gave her an odd look, but Clark and Nathan seemed relieved.

"Yes, dear," Olivia said. "You are welcome to lie down upstairs. I'll take you now."

Olivia shot a glare at Nathan as he tried to help Angel up, obviously meaning for him to step away. Looking bewildered, Nathan complied, and Olivia held out a hand to aid Angel in his place. Then Olivia wrapped an arm around Angel's waist, steadying her as they walked toward the stairs.

When Angel was settled in one of the upstairs rooms, Olivia left, then reappeared holding a cup of water and a biscuit.

"Do you think you can eat this, dear?" Olivia asked.

Angel nodded, sitting up and gratefully accepting Olivia's gift. Fists on her waist, Olivia watched silently as Angel nibbled at the biscuit, then abruptly asked, "Why are you really living with my nephew?"

Angel inhaled rapidly, breathing in a biscuit crumb as she did so, causing her to cough violently. Olivia patiently waited for Angel's coughing spell to subside, then asked, "Well?"

Unsure how to respond, Angel hesitated. She and Nathan had already told Clark and Olivia why Angel was there—what other answer was Olivia looking for? When Angel said nothing, Olivia crossed her arms. "Well then, let me ask you another question. Are you pregnant?"

Angel gaped at Olivia. She shouldn't have known. Even though Angel was nearly four months along, she hadn't begun to show, and she hadn't spoken of it to anyone. But Olivia already seemed to know the truth. She was merely waiting for Angel to confirm it.

Angel whispered, "Yes. But how did you know?"

Olivia waved an impatient hand, as though Angel was trying to distract her from the most important topic at hand. "I have a knack for being able to tell when women are pregnant." She continued in a softer voice, "Is it Nathan's?"

"What?" Angel asked, aghast, then said emphatically, "No."

In a gesture that reminded Angel strikingly of Nathan, Olivia rubbed the bridge of her nose with her fingers. Angel wasn't sure whether Olivia was relieved or upset by her answer. Finally, Olivia asked, "Does Nathan know?"

Again, Angel's voice was small as she answered, "No."

Olivia shook her head, then sighed, suddenly growing almost maternal. "How far along are you?"

"Almost four months."

Olivia raised an eyebrow, glancing at Angel's slight frame as she replied, "And you know this for sure?"

Angel felt her cheeks redden at the implication, and she stared at the floor as she choked out her answer. "Yes."

Olivia paused, then asked, "If not Nathan, then who?"

For the first time since Olivia had begun questioning her, Angel straightened, raised her chin, and met Olivia's eyes without hesitation. "I don't know. I never asked his name, and he never asked permission."

Olivia stared at her for a moment, and then as understanding set in, her eyes widened and her mouth opened in a silent "Oh." Then, "Does Nathan know about that part?"

"Yes."

The two sat in silence. Finally, Olivia asked, "What will you do when the baby comes?"

Angel shrugged, looking helplessly at her hands. "I don't know."

"Will you stay here?"

"I'm leaving on the next train, early next week," Angel whispered.

"What about Nathan?" Olivia asked.

Angel considered Olivia, then said slowly, "What are you asking?"

"Would you leave Nathan?"

Angel met Olivia's gaze evenly. "He's not mine to leave."

"And if he was?"

The strange lightness Angel had been battling came again to her chest at Olivia's words, and she fought to squash it. The idea, the possibility that there could exist something between her and Nathan to leave, something more than just a daydream, filled her with joy. But she hated that joy because she had no hope that the imaginations from which it sprung were real, or could ever be real.

"Why are you asking me these things?" she whispered furiously, keenly aware of the men downstairs.

"My dear, Nathan is a good boy, a good man. I assume you know his father?" Olivia asked. Angel hesitated, and Olivia added, "At least you know of him?" At Angel's nod of affirmation, Olivia continued speaking. "Everything Nathan has ever done has been to make sure he is nothing like his father. I would be . . . most distressed . . . if anything should happen to change that."

Angel spat out the question before she could stop herself. "If you are so distressed by the prospect of Nathan becoming like his father, why did you leave Nathan with him in the first place?"

Olivia nodded, and her eyes seemed tired. "That is a fair question, but one that I cannot answer." She raised her hand as Angel opened her mouth to object. "I agree, Nathan deserves to know, but now is not the time. It would do more harm than good at this moment, I think."

She then shifted the subject. "Nathan deserves to know about your pregnancy as well. I understand your reluctance to tell him, but he may react differently than you think. He is a good man—he takes after Clark more than James in that way at least."

It was something in Olivia's voice, more than her words, that caught Angel's attention, and she looked up. "What do you know of it?"

Angel's question was less a challenge to Olivia's assessment of Nathan's character than it was an inkling of an impossible idea—what had Olivia ever needed to tell Clark? But the idea must not have been so impossible, because Olivia turned from Angel, twisting a handkerchief in her hands.

Angel waited in silence. When Olivia finally turned around, there were tears glittering in her eyes, but none on her delicate cheekbones, and Angel knew that there they would stay. Olivia sat on the edge of the bed, facing Angel, and suddenly Angel was afraid of the words Olivia would speak. Angel opened her mouth to speak, to tell Olivia she was feeling better, to tell her anything so that she would not have to sit with her any longer. Angel could hear the muffled sound of tight voices through the floorboards beneath her, but she knew that even interrupting another of Clark and Nathan's fights would be better than what Olivia was going to say. In the end, it was Olivia's face that held her there. It was filled with a quiet intensity Angel had never before seen in the woman. Angel exhaled, resolving to stay for whatever words Olivia would speak.

"When I was about your age, there were two boys," Olivia began. Her voice was filled with fondness as she continued. "One was my dear friend. He was kind, and honest. The other"—Olivia paused, and when she continued, Angel started at the sudden bitterness that had filled Olivia's voice—"was tall, and handsome, and charming. I thought he was wonderful, and all the other girls my age were positively giddy whenever he was around.

"But he chose me, and that made me feel special. It wasn't long before he had my father's blessing and he had asked for my hand in marriage. On Saturdays, he would pick me up with his team and wagon, and we would go driving. And then, one Saturday . . ." Olivia stared hard at Angel, but Angel knew Olivia wasn't seeing her. Olivia was seeing things in the past.

"Then, one Saturday, my wonderful boy showed his true colors. When he was done, he brought me home and left me on the front porch. And do you know what he said?" Angel held her breath, but Olivia didn't wait for her response. "He told me I'd best get myself put together before my father came home, else my father would be so ashamed of me." Olivia made a choking noise, and Angel's eyes darted to those delicate cheekbones, but though the tears now clung precariously to Olivia's lower lashes, there they stayed.

In a calmer voice, Olivia went on. "I knew that wasn't true. If my father had ever found out, he would have shot that boy dead. But I was so embarrassed and so ashamed. I watched him drive away, and cried, and cried, and cried. My mother and father weren't home from town yet—they had gone to a meeting about the new school, and my two younger sisters had gone with them. It was the other boy—my friend—who found me. He had been planning to leave that Monday to go away to college, so he had stopped by to say goodbye."

Olivia's voice cracked as she spoke the word *goodbye*, and Angel knew the memory of that goodbye still tore at her. Olivia continued. "I wouldn't have told him what happened either, but as soon as he saw me, he knew. I've never seen him so angry, before or since then. He wanted to go after the other boy, but I wouldn't let him. I didn't want anyone to know what happened. I made him promise me."

This time, when Olivia paused, Angel couldn't help herself, and she asked, "What happened?"

Olivia glanced at Angel, perhaps for the first time since she had begun talking, and then motioned to Angel's midriff. "I found myself in much the same situation as you. Except that before anyone else knew, I was married."

Angel felt her muscles tense as she asked, "To the first boy?"

Olivia's face softened. "No," she said, "to my friend. To Clark"

Still, Angel's fingernails dug into her palms. "He married you because you were pregnant with another man's child?"

"No. He married me because he had been in love with me all along."

"Did you love him?"

"I cared for him then. I love him more than anything now."

At Angel's skeptical expression, Olivia added fondly, "Oh, I know he can be rather obstinate, but he's a good man."

Olivia continued. "The other boy hinted to others in town that I must have betrayed his trust with Clark, and soon, that was what everyone believed. They couldn't understand why else I would have married Clark so suddenly when I had been engaged to the other boy. Clark and I left. I wasn't there when James—that's Nathan's father—started seeing Effie, my sister." Olivia choked back a sob, and the tears finally spilled past her lashes onto her cheeks, this time unrestrained. "Effie wrote me about James, and I tried to warn her, but she thought I was jealous. I couldn't convince her otherwise."

Olivia's eyes were distant, remembering. "She always was stubborn that way."

"I still don't understand," Angel said, interrupting Olivia's thoughts. "How could your sister marry Nathan's father?"

Olivia smiled, but the iciness in her eyes was chilling. "He could be charming."

Angel couldn't help shuddering at the chill that had settled in her stomach.

"What happened to the baby?" Angel asked softly.

A strange expression came over Olivia's face. She seemed unsure of how to respond. When she finally did, she spoke only one word. "Felicity."

"Oh!" Angel exclaimed. Then, as the implications chased away her initial shock, she whispered again softly, "Oh." She began to ask the first question that came to her mind. "Clark—"

Olivia cut Angel off. "He treats her like she was his own daughter."

They sat in silence for a moment. The air felt heavy, and trying to lighten it, Angel changed the subject with the first thought that came to her mind.

"Nathan thinks his mother was unfaithful to his father, and that's why his father killed her," Angel said. It seemed odd that adultery and death could be lighter topics than those that had preceded them.

Shocked from her reverie by Angel's words, Olivia studied her for a long moment, then asked, "Does Nathan truly believe James killed Effie?"

Angel nodded.

"Did he say why he thought that?" Olivia's eyes were intense.

"He said he had heard enough rumors to make a guess at the truth."

The intensity faded from Olivia, and she nodded to herself as though that was the answer she had expected.

"I've heard those rumors as well, but nothing more substantiated." Olivia made a sound of disgust. "No one knows anything, but everyone wants to believe they know something."

"Do you think Effie really would have been unfaithful to him?" Angel asked.

Olivia said thoughtfully, "No, I don't think so. Effie never was particularly discreet. She liked attention, and she was always a bit of a flirt. If James was not paying attention to her, it is easy to believe she would have sought that elsewhere—an innocent lark, she would have called it. But even if she was unhappy with James, I don't believe she ever would have been unfaithful to him. Whether James would have believed that, though, is an entirely different story."

Despite how she had encouraged Nathan to speak with Clark and Olivia, Angel couldn't keep a note of indignation from entering her voice as she asked her next question. "And even knowing all that about Nathan's father—about James—you believed it was best to leave him here?"

Olivia started to speak, but Angel cut her off with a shake of her head. "I know you won't tell me the reasons why you left Nathan here, but can you at least tell me why you're here now?"

Olivia looked down at her hands. "Nelle—the doctor's wife—and I were childhood friends. She never did believe the rumors that were spread about Clark and me. She writes me from time to time with news of her family and Nathan. That's how Clark and I found out James had disappeared."

"Is that why you came back?"

"Well, yes, partially," Olivia said. As Angel raised an eyebrow, Olivia added, "Felicity had also recently accepted a teaching position at a school farther west, and the combination of the two factors made it seem a good time . . ." Olivia's voice trailed off, then she hastily added, almost pleading, "It's different than how it sounds though. We did—we do—care for Nathan. It's just . . . James is predictable in many ways, but he often makes threats, and it is impossible to know whether he will follow through on them. I only know a few details of the conversation that preceded it—Clark refuses to speak of it—but while we were here for Effie's funeral, James told Clark that he would kill all of us—Nathan, Clark, Felicity, and I—before he would let Nathan leave with us."

Olivia's eyes grew distant again, remembering. "In front of all those people, just like that, James pulled Clark aside, all casual-like so he wouldn't draw attention. Smiling the whole time, he started asking Clark about Felicity—"How was she doing?" and "Remind him again how long after we'd been married that little girl was born." He acted like a concerned older brother, wanting to know if Clark was sure the baby was his, or "Hadn't I been spending my time with some other man before we were married?" And then he told Clark that if we tried to take Nathan with us, he'd shoot all three of us. Everyone else was out of earshot, so it looked to them like brothers reconciling after a tragedy."

Olivia's face was a mask of disgust, an expression Angel knew she herself mirrored. Finally, Angel asked, "How could Clark stand there with James and act as though nothing was wrong?"

"Oh." Olivia chuckled darkly. "Believe me. Clark did not act as though nothing was wrong. I didn't know what they were talking about—I was on the other side of the room—but I knew it was worse than we had anticipated before we made the decision to go to Effie's funeral. Clark stood there, his face going all purple-red. I think the red was from him being angry, and the purple was because he was holding his breath trying to keep from doing or saying something that would get us both into trouble. James stood there, calm as could be. At the time, everyone thought James was the brother trying to do the right thing and mend rifts with his wayward brother. Clark looked like the black sheep of the family."

Then, suddenly without a trace of even her dark humor remaining, Olivia turned her full attention to Angel, facing her straight on as though to make sure Angel caught and understood the full gravity of the words she would speak. "Everything Clark has ever done has been to protect Felicity and I. Clark was trying to protect us this time as well—all of us, even Nathan."

Angel nodded slowly, then asked, "Do you think James would really have followed through with his threat?"

"I don't know. He'd been drinking, and that was always when he was the most dangerous. But as for following through on a threat he'd made when he'd been drinking?" Olivia shook her head. "It's hard to say."

Angel paused, then said incredulously, "Is this the reason you wouldn't tell me—why you stayed away, or is there more?"

Olivia refused to meet Angel's eyes. "There is another reason, but Clark would not want Nathan to know of James's threat either. He believes it's one thing to be the son of a drunk, to be beaten by your father, but another to know your father threatened to kill you without a second thought."

Angel thought for a moment. "What about the rumors of him murdering Nathan's mother? Wouldn't James have drawn attention at the funeral because of those?"

"Yes, well," Olivia said grimly. "I think it was much easier for people to give him the benefit of the doubt before he became a drunkard who openly beat his son. I don't think so many people believed the rumors at that point."

"Did you believe them?" Angel asked.

"I hadn't heard them until we came back for the funeral, and even then, it was only a whisper as I passed by. I thought I must have misheard. I didn't want them to be true."

"You wanted to give James the benefit of the doubt?" Angel asked skeptically.

Olivia shook her head vehemently, her eyes growing steely. "Make no mistake, there is no love lost between James and myself. No, I didn't—I still don't—want to believe he could have killed her, not because I care for James in any way, but because Effie was my sister, and I loved her. If James killed her, then in part I blame myself for not doing more to prevent their marriage."

Angel opened her mouth to ask another question, but Olivia gently interrupted her. "I think that is enough questions for now. Don't you think we had best go save Nathan and Clark from each other?"

Olivia tilted her head at the door, listening, and stepped toward the sound of voices that were not raised but tight. She stopped, exasperated.

"Oh, for heaven's sake, they make talking about the weather sound like torture."

Angel hesitated, then asked, "You came back in part because Nathan's father disappeared. How can you be so sure he won't come back?"

Olivia paused, hand on the door latch, then said, "I am sure of many things—that the sun will rise in the east tomorrow, that Clark loves me—"

She eyed Angel, then added, "That Nathan cares for you, even if he hasn't realized it yet." Angel flushed. Olivia continued. "There are no sureties where James is concerned. I would like to believe that he will never come back. But it is easier for me to convince myself he had nothing to do with Effie's death than it is for me to believe he is gone for good. James has done very little for good in his life."

With that, Olivia pushed open the door. Angel stood motionless, unable to shake the heaviness that had settled into her stomach. For the first time since she had first stepped in its walls, the thought of Nathan's cabin didn't fill her with feelings of safety.

Olivia hesitated, resting her hand on the doorjamb. She then turned and laid a hand on Angel's shoulder. "Please know that should circumstances change, you are welcome to stay with us for as long as you need."

Olivia's kind offer caught Angel off guard. She found herself nodding her thanks before she had thought about Olivia's words and following her downstairs to where Clark and Nathan sat tolerating one another.

Nathan looked relieved to see her, and he rose to his feet as she walked into the room.

"I'm fine," Angel reassured him, and he smiled back.

NATHAN WAS RELIEVED when they finally stood to leave. Supper had passed pleasantly enough, with Clark and Nathan even managing to find a neutral topic neither of them cared enough about to argue over. Admittedly, their discussion of the intricacies of wood grain had nearly put both Olivia and Angel to sleep.

Now, Nathan and Angel stood at the door to leave. Olivia reached out and touched Angel on the arm. "If it's fine with you, dear, I'd like to pay you a visit tomorrow, just to make sure you are feeling well."

Angel smiled. "I am feeling fine, but I would welcome the visit."

Returning Angel's smile, Olivia nodded. "Tomorrow it is, then."

As Nathan and Angel were walking to the wagon, Angel suddenly stopped, raising a hand to her neck. "My necklace. The clasp must have come loose when I was lying down upstairs." Angel's eyes widened. "I need to find it before we leave. It was my mother's."

Nathan laid a hand on her arm. "I'll run upstairs and find it."

Angel started to protest, and Nathan interrupted her with a grin. "It will take less time if I do it—if you go in, you will stop and start talking to Olivia again."

Angel sighed, then nodded, and Nathan walked back into Clark and Olivia's house.

Startled, Olivia looked up from an object she was cradling in her hands.

"Angel lost her necklace. She thinks it's upstairs," Nathan explained.

"Oh, of course. You are welcome to look," Olivia said distractedly.

Nathan found the necklace easily and returned downstairs the same way he had come—taking the stairs two at a time. When he reached the ground floor, his attention was drawn yet again by Olivia, who was now sitting at the kitchen table, still holding something in her hands.

"Olivia?" Nathan asked. Startled, Olivia looked up. Nathan gestured toward her hands. "What are you holding?" he asked.

Olivia smiled sadly, then turned her hand palm up and uncurled her fingers. She was holding a large piece of the broken platter. "Your mother gave me this when Clark and I were married."

Looking intently at the shard, Nathan spoke softly. "I know." The two stood in silence for a moment, then Nathan said, "You said it wasn't important."

Olivia glanced at him. "Your mother was—is—important. But the platter was only a reminder of her. Angel is here now, and therefore, she is more important than a broken serving dish, no matter what memories are associated with the dish."

For the first time, Nathan felt something like gratitude toward his aunt. "Thank you," he said.

Olivia nodded, and Nathan exited through the door for the second time that night.

When he came out, Angel asked anxiously, "What took so long? Did you find it?"

Nathan handed Angel her necklace. "Nah, I found it quick. I just started talking to Olivia."

Angel hid a smile behind her hand. Nathan chose to ignore the motion.

SILVERY CLOUDS of mist rose from their mouths and noses as they traveled, the moonlight reflecting off the warmth they breathed. Angel interrupted the silence first.

"What did you and Clark talk about while I was upstairs?"

"The weather, mostly. He seems to think we're due for another storm."

"Do you think he's right?"

"I don't know," Nathan said, then added under his breath, "I hope not."

Angel wasn't sure whether Nathan's lack of enthusiasm was due to the prospect of another snowstorm, or the idea of Clark being right.

"What about you and Olivia?" Nathan asked.

Angel opened her mouth to reply, then realized that even if it were possible for her to tell Nathan what she and Olivia had spoken of without breaking strict confidences, it wouldn't be possible to condense even the main points of their conversation into an appropriate response. She shrugged and replied lamely, "Many things. Not the weather."

Nathan didn't press. They traveled wordlessly until the cabin came into view, and Angel couldn't resist asking the question pressing on her mind.

"What if he comes back?"

"What if who comes back?" Nathan answered, bewildered.

"Your father, James."

Nathan was silent for a moment, then turned to Angel. "Where did you hear my father's name? I never told you."

"Olivia told me."

"You two must have covered a pretty wide range of topics. You asked Olivia about my father?"

"Well, no, not exactly. She brought him up."

Nathan eyed Angel. "And why did she bring up my father?"

"She told me that you weren't like him."

Nathan didn't seem to know how to respond and did not reply. Finally, Angel broke the silence again and asked, "Did you know your father threatened to kill them—and you—if they tried to take you with them?"

Nathan's grip on the reins tightened, and he let out a long breath of air. "No. I didn't know that. When did this happen?"

"At your mother's funeral."

"Of course he did," Nathan said bitterly, almost to himself.

He turned his attention back to Angel. "Why would Olivia tell you this?"

"I asked her why they came back."

"You asked point-blank, and she told you? Just like that?"

"Well," Angel hesitated, "yes and no. Yes, I asked and she told me, but it was not 'just like that.'" Angel sighed and hoped Nathan wouldn't press as she explained, "There was an entire conversation that led up to it."

Nathan shrugged. "If you say so."

"Clark didn't want you to know. He told Olivia it would be worse for you to know your father threatened to kill you."

Nathan's expression, which had darkened at Angel's first words, seemed to soften slightly as she finished speaking, although a trace of the anger still remained in his eyes. He shook his head in disgust. "That's just like Clark," he grumbled, "always thinking he knows what's best for someone else."

But even though Nathan's words were gruff, Angel could tell that Clark's sentiment had struck a chord. For the first time since his aunt and uncle's return, Nathan seemed just a little bit lighter, rather than weighed down, after the mention of Clark's name.

Nathan shook his head. "Every time I think my father can't get any worse, he manages to prove me wrong. Impressive, given that he's not even here."

"What happens if your father does come back?" Angel asked.

The wagon came to a stop as they pulled up next to the cabin. Nathan turned to face her.

"I don't know what will happen if he comes back. I hope he never does. But if he does and you're still here"—Nathan paused, holding her eyes—"I promise I won't let him hurt you."

Angel nodded slowly. She climbed carefully from the wagon seat and, pausing midway down, reached out a hand to touch Nathan's, still outstretched from helping her from the wagon seat.

"Thank you," she said softly.

"For what?"

"For everything."

Nathan nodded silently, watching as Angel walked toward the cabin, making sure she made it inside safely before he pulled the horses forward to unhitch them from the wagon and brush them down. Just before she closed the door behind her, she saw Nathan's gaze move thoughtfully down to land on the hand she had touched, and he drew his thumb across the knuckles of his fingers where hers had brushed his.

Angel was awake when Nathan returned from the barn. The comforting sound of boots on the wooden floor came closer and then paused, hesitating as though Nathan was deciding whether to knock on her door. But no knock came, and again she heard the sound of boots on the floor, growing softer as they moved away.

12

---

nd then there was Effie. I wanted to care for her. I did care for
her. I made sure I wasn't ever drinking around her. I know
people warned her, but I've heard it said love is blind. In her
case, it was both blind and deaf.

❧

NATHAN WALKED INTO THE STORE, nodding a greeting to the
storekeeper as he strode through the door. The cabin's supply of flour
and sugar was running low, so Nathan had gone into town to
purchase those, along with a few other sundries—kerosene for the
lantern, ammunition, molasses, thread, and the like. Whether he
agreed with him on other matters was questionable, but Nathan had
to admit Clark had a decent sense of the weather. If Clark said there
was another storm coming—and he had—Nathan wanted to be well
stocked when it came.

Besides, Olivia was visiting Angel back at the cabin, and as much
as he hated to admit it, Nathan felt better knowing someone, even if it
was Olivia, was with Angel while he was gone.

Nathan shook his head. The two had formed a strange bond that he didn't understand, and even if only for Angel's sake, Nathan would have tried to be friendly toward Olivia regardless. But seeing Olivia hold so tightly to the piece of the serving dish her sister—Nathan's mother—had turned a switch inside Nathan. He no longer felt the bitterness toward his aunt, or even his uncle, that he had carried for years.

"... that Evans boy."

Nathan's attention was drawn back to his surroundings as he heard his last name at the end of a whispered sentence. Slowly, he turned to see the source of the whispers. It was Nelle Davis, the doctor's wife, and her niece, Valentine. Nathan groaned softly to himself. It was Valentine, of course, who was speaking. Nelle's face was pinched, and she seemed to be biting her tongue—whether she was refraining from speaking against himself or Valentine, Nathan could not tell.

As he struggled between confronting the women or quietly exiting the store before anyone else could recognize him, snippets of the conversation wove their way through the store goods and to his ears.

"... come to church ... living with him ... who does she think she is ... doesn't even have the decency to act embarrassed ..."

Nathan's ears burned, and he was grateful Angel was not with him to hear Valentine's words. He had just made up his mind to quietly exit when Nelle spoke. She didn't bother to whisper.

"Oh, come now, my dear. What if there is a perfectly good explanation for all this? Perhaps they are relatives."

Valentine sniffed. "They don't look related."

"Well, perhaps there is another explanation. Perhaps we should be thinking how kind Nathan is to help someone in need."

Valentine hmphed. "Perhaps," she mimicked her aunt, "he is too kind, and she is too willing to be helped. Whatever trouble she is in that she might need help out of, I'm sure she brought it on herself. It's shameful, really."

The flame in Nathan's ears moved to his face, but the flush was no longer from embarrassment. It was from anger. He wanted to tell the truth to this thoughtless girl, to try to make her understand even though he knew she wouldn't. He stepped into the aisle, behind Valentine but into Nelle's line of vision. Before he could open his mouth, Nelle met his eyes and spoke again.

"Child," she said firmly to Valentine, and the title was no term of endearment, "you have much to learn of people, and life, and love, and kindness. Let's have no more of this silliness."

Then, she nodded hello to Nathan.

He nodded back. "Afternoon, Mrs. Davis, Miss Thomas."

Valentine had the grace to blush as she turned to face Nathan. She had once tried to flirt with him when her parents weren't watching. Now, she tried to smile sweetly at him, but her smile faltered uncertainly when he failed to smile back. He'd had little patience, then and now, for Valentine's games.

He excused himself, but as he passed the two women, he hoped Nelle saw the gratitude he was trying to silently convey with his eyes.

NATHAN WAS CONSIDERABLY MORE cheerful on his return to the cabin than he had been when he had left. When he arrived, he was surprised to find Angel and Olivia outside, standing next to another wagon—Clark was there.

"I know Olivia walked here this morning," Clark explained hurriedly as Nathan pulled up beside him, "but I thought with the storm coming, it would be best if I picked Olivia up."

Nathan nodded curtly. "Shows good sense. I'd think you were a fool if you had taken a chance with her getting caught in a blizzard like the one we had a few weeks back."

Clark eyed Nathan, but didn't reply. Nathan turned his attention to Angel.

"Are you still feeling well?" he asked.

Angel, smiling, nodded. "I just needed some rest."

In that instant, Nathan couldn't help disliking Olivia less. The Angel standing outside in the sunlight almost reminded him of the

Angel he had seen in the meadow the day before the first winter storm came—somehow lighter, unburdened and happy. Beautiful.

"I hate to leave when you've only just made it back, Nathan, but I think we'd best be heading home before the storm hits," Olivia interrupted his thoughts.

Nathan nodded his agreement. "It's not bad out there yet, but I think Clark had it right. There's clouds starting to show on the horizon. They don't look like they're moving fast, but I'd guess the storm will hit us before nightfall."

Olivia laid a hand on Angel's shoulder. "Take care of yourself."

As Olivia passed Nathan on her way to the wagon, she spoke quietly so only Nathan could hear. "Make sure you keep an eye on her."

Startled, Nathan glanced back at Angel, then nodded his agreement.

When she saw that Nathan would do as she asked, Olivia smiled again and walked to the wagon. Clark helped her step up and then turned to say goodbye. Nathan, who had followed Olivia's path as she walked back to the wagon, stretched out his hand and said, "Travel safely. I hope you can make it back in good time."

Shock spread across Clark's face, but to his credit, he stretched out his hand to clasp Nathan's in his own almost immediately. Olivia hid a smile behind her hand, but by the time Clark looked at her in question, the expression had disappeared. The moment passed almost as soon as it had begun, and the two released their handshake, stepping back as though nothing had happened. They all waved their goodbyes, and Clark and Olivia set off at a brisk pace.

Nathan walked back to Angel. Even though she claimed to be feeling better, she still looked tired. As he and Angel went inside the cabin, Nathan saw that Olivia had been kind enough to start supper while she had been there, and he felt another wave of gratitude toward her rush over him.

Angel sat with her elbows on the table, chin resting on her hands. Her hair was braided so loosely behind her that it was almost falling out of its binding.

Nathan sat across from her and asked, "Did you enjoy your visit with Olivia?"

Angel smiled. "Yes, it was nice. I wish you could like Clark and Olivia better. I don't mind seeing them, but I know it bothers you."

"Olivia is growing on me," Nathan admitted.

"Really?" Angel asked curiously. "Why is that?"

"I don't know. She's been good to you these last couple weeks—especially yesterday and today—and I guess that makes me think that they can't be all bad. Or at least Olivia can't be," he answered.

Angel shifted in her chair, and as she did, a tress of hair came loose from her braid, falling around her face. Nathan's instinctive reaction seemed so natural that he followed it without thought. He raised his hand to brush the hair back from Angel's face before he knew what he was doing, then froze, hand in midair.

He wanted to kiss her.

Nathan felt the heat rise in his face and jerked back as the realization hit him. *Ah . . .*

Angel looked at him strangely, and Nathan realized his strangled exclamation had not remained silently in his head. He scrambled backward, and the chair he had been sitting on toppled as he hurriedly rose to his feet. Suddenly all of his movements seemed painfully clumsy, and he retrieved the chair and set it right side up with exaggerated care.

"I forgot something," he offered in explanation. "In the barn. I need to go take care of it."

"Right now?" Angel asked, confused. "What did you forget?"

"Ah, something, nothing important. I just need to go. I'll be back."

As Nathan spoke, he slipped his arms into the sleeves of his coat and walked to the door. Unable to meet Angel's gaze, he lifted the latch and bolted. He didn't look back. He didn't want to see the confusion in Angel's eyes. He was afraid if he saw it, he would want to explain it away.

The walk to the barn was too short. Once he had closed the door behind himself, Nathan found himself pacing nervously back and forth from one end of the barn to the other. There were no cows to be milked, no hay to be pitched, no harnesses to be mended. He was tempted to break something just so he would have something to fix.

Nathan didn't know how he had been caught so off guard. He hadn't seen it coming. It had been easy to dismiss—of course he cared about Angel. Her memory had been with him, for better or worse, since he was twelve. Seven years ago, she had given him hope. Now, seven years later, she had given him belonging.

All of that and more, he could rationalize and dismiss into the realms of friendship. Wanting to kiss Angel, well, that was a different story. He couldn't explain that away.

And worse, it had suddenly struck Nathan that he didn't want Angel to leave.

Nathan exhaled deeply and ran a hand through his hair. He remembered clearly Angel's response when he had first asked her to stay—she had been terrified, assuming he had been asking something of her she was unwilling to give, even though he had only meant to offer aid. He didn't want Angel to feel as though he expected something of her in return for what she called his "kindness."

Nathan had asked Angel to stay purely with the intent of helping her, but he couldn't deny that the reasons he hoped she would stay had moved beyond a simple desire to return a seven-year-old favor. He felt selfish for hoping she would stay. Angel had told him she wanted to go someplace where no one knew her. What kind of life could she have in this town? Certainly not one of anonymity. And as much as he denied the possibility, part of him wondered what would happen if his father ever returned. Nathan could not ask Angel to care for him. He would not ask her to stay.

When he returned to the cabin, Angel was already in her room, and Nathan was relieved that he wouldn't need to explain, at least immediately, his sudden exit to Angel. Still, his relief didn't last long, and he found himself lying in bed fully clothed, hands behind his head, listening to the howling wind of the growing storm outside and staring at the ceiling late into the night.

THIS TIME, the storm lasted upwards of three days. The icy winds packed the swirling snow into drifts, and by the second day, Nathan knew that even if the storm stopped before the train was scheduled to arrive, he and Angel wouldn't be able to make it into town.

Nathan's sense of relief was tempered by the guilt he felt over his relief; that same guilt was tempered by the lack of concern Angel had shown when Nathan had informed her that they were, once again, stranded by the snow. If anything, Angel had seemed relieved as well.

Nathan thought of the words Angel had spoken when he had first offered her a place to stay: "When you wake up tomorrow morning, will you wish you could pretend today was only a dream, or will you want to believe it was real?"

The words had seemed strange to Nathan when Angel had first spoken them, but now they seemed to fit better than any other words Nathan could think of. He couldn't shake the feeling that he and Angel were living inside an illusion of peace and safety that might come crashing down at any moment. And Nathan had not yet decided whether, when reality forced its way into their small piece of the world, he would turn away and let his and Angel's time fade like the dream he knew it was or fight to hold on to the reality they had created for themselves.

FOR THE FIRST time since she had arrived at the cabin, Angel woke before Nathan.

Up until now, she had only occasionally felt faint flutters of movement. At first the flutters had terrified her, an additional confirmation of the thing she already knew. Gradually, she had grown accustomed to the tiny movements, and eventually, she had begun to welcome them, learning their patterns—how they always grew more frequent after Angel had eaten a meal or when she lay down to sleep at night. But this was the first time the movements had progressed to anything beyond a flutter, even waking Angel from her sleep, and she felt a smile cross her face as she looked at the place where her hand lay.

She had opened the door from her room, expecting from the silence in the other room that Nathan had already begun taking care of the chores in the barn, and found Nathan breathing deeply, still asleep in his bed. At the sound of the opening door, Nathan stirred, stretching as he woke. When he realized Angel was in the room, he sat up with a start.

"Is everything okay?" he asked.

"I am fine, but I could ask you the same," Angel answered. "You are usually up long before I am."

Nathan shook his head slowly, propping himself up with one hand and rubbing his eyes with the other.

"I'm fine. I—what?"

His hair was sticking out on the side, and the corner of Angel's mouth turned upward.

"It's nothing," Angel answered, still smiling, then turned the conversation. "I know it's early, but I wanted to talk to you about something."

"What's that?"

Angel crossed the room to sit on the edge of the bed and faced Nathan, then as an expression of supreme discomfort crossed his face, Angel stood again. She stood uncertainly, fidgeting with her hands, and even though she recognized it and hated it and fought it, her shoulders tensed and hunched protectively forward. "I'm sorry."

Nathan shook his head, motioning for her to sit again. "Nah, it's fine. Please sit. I don't mind. It's just you caught me off guard. Sometimes I forget you grew up where that sort of familiarity doesn't mean anything."

Angel felt her face tighten and her cheeks redden. Even though she knew Nathan hadn't intended his words to be insulting, she was not sure that wasn't exactly what they had been. His words punctured the confidence that had bubbled inside her, and fear began to creep into her chest, displacing the calm she had felt. Sternly, she pushed the creeping iciness into the smallest corner and, breathing deeply, pulled a chair from the table to sit beside the bed, trying to convince herself again that talking to Nathan—telling him of her pregnancy—was the right decision.

She looked up at Nathan, who was watching her curiously, then back at her stomach as she felt the baby kick again. A warm feeling crept over her, and in an instant, her decision was made. This was a secret she could keep no longer.

Angel took a deep breath. "There's something I need to tell you."

Nathan must have felt her nervousness, because he seemed to grow more guarded, leaning back slightly. Angel's heart started pounding in her chest, and the comfortable warmth left her body. She grew cold. Her teeth clenched so tightly against the shivers that had suddenly seized her entire body she could hardly speak, but she forced the words out. Nathan had moved toward her as she started shaking, but she shook her head without looking at him and he sat back.

"The morning . . . the morning I was attacked . . . there's more. And I knew—I've known for a long time, but at first there was no reason to tell you, and then when there was I was afraid to tell you. I didn't know how, and I'm sorry . . ."

Nathan looked so uneasy at this point that Angel nearly couldn't finish, but she forced the last words out in a whisper. "I'm pregnant."

Then she buried her face in her hands.

Nathan's mouth opened slightly, and he shook his head. He looked away, then back at Angel as though to convince himself he had heard correctly, then away again.

"Pregnant?" he asked. Angel nodded a confirmation.

Nathan leaned back, closing his eyes and running a hand through his hair. "Oh, this is not good."

And though she understood Nathan's words could have sprung from a multitude of places, they stung a piece of Angel she hadn't even known existed. Unwelcome tears sprang to her eyes, and she blinked violently against them.

"Not good?" Angel asked, her voice cracking. "Not good for who? Me? Or you?"

"Not good for anyone. You know what everyone will think. You know you won't be able to stay once people find out."

Struck, Angel sat back in her chair, the shock of the hurt driving tears from her eyes, but only momentarily. Tears slid down her face as she whispered, "That is why I was leaving—why I wanted to go somewhere no one knew me. But I had started to hope I wouldn't have to."

For a moment, Nathan looked as though he was going to come to her, but then he shook his head and threw the covers back, standing abruptly. "I'm sorry," he said, "but I can't talk about this right now. I'll be back."

He pulled on his boots and coat, hat and gloves while Angel watched in silence. About to open the door, Nathan paused, looking back at Angel. She thought he must have seen the reflection of her broken heart in her eyes, because his face grew pinched and he spoke haltingly, "Please . . . don't . . . don't take me leaving as me being angry with you. I just . . . I need to get some air. I need to think."

He opened the door and stepped out before he could see Angel's reaction. His boots crunched as he stepped out into the snow—a testament to the frigid air outside—and the cold draft from the open door struck Angel. It didn't matter. Her body already felt like ice.

NATHAN STRODE through the white snow, ignoring the bite of the freezing air on his cheeks. He didn't know where he was going, only that he needed to be away from that cabin. He didn't know what he was thinking. Well, that was not true. He had been thinking of Angel and little else the past few days. What he didn't know was how he had let himself come to think of her in that way.

They had spent the past few days snowed in, with Nathan leaving only to take care of the barn chores each morning and evening. Those few days had been filled with laughter and warm firelight. Angel had taught him to play checkers—a game he had never had much use for up until now. Nathan had watched her—she had almost glowed in the firelight—and a few times she had caught his eye and smiled shyly back at his sheepish grin.

The memory caught in his chest and he halted his steps, looking around himself for the first time. He had walked farther than he had intended. Nathan let out a soft growl of frustration, then turned and began the long walk home. As he walked, this time with greater and greater purpose, the thoughts that had been swirling in his mind became more and more solid.

Whatever else happened, he knew he didn't want Angel to leave. He cared for her, cared for her in a way he knew was more than friendship or gratitude. He had felt those things—and still felt them —for Angel. But this, even though it had crept up on Nathan so subtly he hadn't noticed until it was fully upon him, this was different.

He cared for Angel, and he would tell her he cared. He would make her understand that he didn't expect anything—that she was free to go or stay no matter what, but he had made his decision. It was time to give Angel the chance to make hers.

SOMETHING about the approaching crunch of boots on snow was wrong, but Angel was too relieved by the sound of Nathan's approach to pay it any mind. It felt like hours that he had been gone. She used a rag to finish drying the dish she was holding and wiped her hands on her skirt, turning as the door creaked open. "Nathan—" she began, then froze.

There were three men standing in the doorway. The first was obviously the leader; the two in the rear looked to him as they saw Angel standing in the room.

The leader said, "Where is Nathan?"

Nathan was out getting some air, whatever that meant. He had already been gone longer than Angel had expected. Angel spoke carefully, deliberately vague. As she spoke, she moved so that the table was fully between herself and the men. "I'm not sure. Nearby. Can I help you?"

The men grinned at each other knowingly.

The leader turned his smile to Angel. "Well, now, I think you can. The boys and me"—he gestured toward the two men at his sides— "were hoping you could do for us some of what you've been doing for our friend Nathan."

Angel kept her face neutral as she replied, "You mean milking cows and mending buttons? Because if so, I would love to help, but I'm sorry—I have more than enough work to keep me busy."

The grins faded off the faces of the men in the rear, and they looked uncertainly toward their leader for direction. He smiled. His lip curled, and his nostrils flared slightly. "Oh, I don't think that's all you've been doing."

Fear crept up Angel's spine and into the base of her skull, emptying it of all thought but defending herself. *Lie*, screamed the voice in the back of her head. So she lied as she cast her eyes frantically around the small room, searching for something, anything to protect herself.

"Nathan will be here soon," Angel said, her voice a half step higher than normal.

"I don't think so." As one, they moved a step closer.

"He was just out in the barn."

"We didn't see him there."

They came closer.

Angel's thoughts were flying so fast she could barely latch on to any of them—her mind processing every detail around her, trying to find some way to stop what was coming. Her ears rang with the sound of blood pounding in her ears. She must have been breathing, but she could no longer feel the air in her chest.

And still they came closer.

Angel backed away, and as she did so, her foot caught on the chair she had pulled next to Nathan's bed that morning, sending her falling heavily to the floor. She cried out, raising a hand to her abdomen and lowering her head. Taking Angel's gesture as one of submission, the leader smiled. As he faced her across the table and the two men flanked her on either side, a tiny movement caught Angel's eye, and she looked past them to see Nathan standing in the open doorway, his eyes icier than the freezing air that swirled into the cabin.

"Nathan," she whispered. The sound barely made it past her lips. Maybe she hadn't been breathing after all—she barely had air to speak.

"I don't think so," the leader said, reaching for her.

He froze as a shotgun cocked behind him.

"I would believe her, if I were you." Nathan's voice drifted through the entrance.

As one, the three men slowly turned to face Nathan. The two on the sides raised their hands, palms facing outward.

"We don't want no trouble—" one of them said but was cut off abruptly as the barrel of the shotgun moved slightly in his direction.

"No trouble? Is that what you call this? Trespassing. Threatening a lady—"

"She ain't a lady, she's a whore—" the leader interrupted, then fell silent as the barrel of the shotgun turned back toward him.

"I'd be careful what you say right about now," Nathan said softly. He caught Angel's eyes and jerked his head to the side, motioning her to move out from behind the table. She did as he asked, slowly edging toward the side of the room. As she did so, Nathan moved to position himself between her and the three men, never taking his attention off them. When he was fully between Angel and the men, he said again, "Get out."

The men backed toward the open door. The leader paused as he stood in the door frame, lips parted though he was going to say something, then reconsidered as he eyed the gun aimed in his direction. Instead, he met Angel's eyes one last time and then let his eyes wander deliberately downward from there.

"Ray," Nathan said, "you're forgetting who I am."

The smirk on Ray's face wavered. He recovered quickly, and the sneer settled back on his lips. "And what is that supposed to mean?"

But Ray had faltered, and even with his forced bravado, Angel could see that he knew he had lost this battle, even before Nathan replied.

"It means that if you ever come back, if you ever hurt her, if you ever even speak to her again . . . if you ever give me a reason, there won't be anywhere you can go to hide, and I won't think twice before pulling this trigger. I am my father's son. This is your last warning. Get out now."

Nathan's finger tightened almost imperceptibly on the trigger. Ray, suddenly paler, licked his lips and backed out the door. He shot one last look back at Angel, and then he was gone.

Nathan walked to the door and raised a hand to push it closed, but something seemed to catch his attention and make him pause in his movement. He hesitated only a moment before closing the door, but in that brief moment, Angel saw him begin to raise the gun before shaking his head and lowering it again.

The motion sent a chill down Angel's back as she recognized what she had just seen for the internal struggle it was. She couldn't be sure, but she thought Nathan had only barely restrained himself from firing after the backs of the men who had come to the cabin.

Then the door closed, and the embers of the fire flickered in the fireplace, again warming the room, and the only sound was that of Nathan setting the gun down by the door and striding across the floor to Angel. For once, he didn't hesitate to touch her, and Angel didn't hesitate to let him as he took her in his arms and held her while she sobbed.

After Angel's breathing had steadied, Nathan led her over to the fireplace and began stirring the fire, then pulled a chair over for Angel to sit. Angel sat, face in hands, as Nathan added one log and then another to the fire.

With an abrupt movement, Angel looked up from her hands. "What is wrong with me?" Her voice cracked as she spoke. She shuddered violently, cold, even though she was sitting next to a blazing fire.

"Angel—" Nathan said, but Angel cut him off as he tried to comfort her.

"Don't say that."

"What?" Nathan asked her, bewildered.

"Stop saying my name. I hate my name," Angel said bitterly.

Nathan paused, and Angel thought he would reach across to her. She braced herself, unconsciously clenching her hands and drawing them closer to her body, then attempted to mask the motion by holding a hand to her abdomen as the muscles in her back tightened. Nathan, however, did not try take her hand. Instead he spoke quietly.

"Angel—"

Angel glowered at him as he repeated her name once more, but Nathan ignored her and continued firmly. "There is nothing wrong with you. It's, just, people assume things."

Angel lifted her head to object, and he hastily added, "The wrong things."

"How does that make a difference? Even if the things they assumed were true, that doesn't make what they were going to do any better."

"No," Nathan admitted, "it doesn't."

They sat in silence. Angel glanced at Nathan. He was looking away, watching the fire dart and dance and flicker. Without taking his eyes from the flames, he said, "I'm sorry I left this morning."

The dull pain that had gripped Angel's chest since Nathan had walked out the door throbbed again, constricting her lungs and making it difficult to breathe. Nathan continued. "I didn't know how to handle it. I still don't. Everything those men assumed, everything everyone assumes—it will only get worse when people realize that you're pregnant."

As her eyes began to tear, Angel forced herself to breathe evenly and to stare straight ahead, unblinking. The room grew watery, blurry.

Nathan's reaction to the news of her pregnancy had wounded her more than she could have expressed, even if she had wanted to, and the apologies he poured out held the sting of salt. She trusted his sincerity. But she didn't believe he could apologize for what had wounded her most, because he didn't seem to realize the unspoken message his words had conveyed: now that he knew Angel was pregnant, there was a time limit on the generosity of Nathan's offer of sanctuary.

"I can't stay here any longer," Angel said abruptly.

Nathan looked taken aback, then hurt. "What? Where will you go?"

Angel hesitated, then said, "Olivia offered to let me stay with them if I ever needed. I will ask her if I may stay with them for a time until I have made other arrangements."

Other arrangements to leave.

"And if you aren't able to stay with them?"

Angel shrugged uncomfortably, and they both knew the answer to Nathan's question—if she couldn't stay with Clark and Olivia, then she wouldn't stay at all.

"But why?" Nathan blurted. "If it's because of what happened today, I will do better. I should have been here to protect you. I shouldn't have left you alone. I should have been here."

Angel shook her head. "You can't protect me all the time. You can't leave everything to take else care of itself while you stand guard for me. It's like what you said—me living here—people assume all the wrong things, and some of them think it gives them the right to treat me however they want. You can't change that, Nathan."

Nathan was silent for a moment, then said, "What if I could?"

"What do you mean?"

Nathan was quiet for so long, Angel began to wonder whether he had had an idea at all, or if his question had been rhetorical, or if he had merely spoken out loud by accident.

Then, he said, "Marry me."

Angel felt the air leave her lungs like it had been sucked out. Once when she was younger—long before her parents had been killed in the steamboat explosion—she had fallen out of a tree she had been climbing and landed flat on her back. This felt the same. She couldn't move. She couldn't breathe. Her mouth opened partially, hanging there for a moment before she gathered her thoughts enough to close it. Words. Normally when she couldn't speak, she felt like she was choking on them, but this time they were just gone. There were no words left to speak, and no air left to form them.

"I know this seems out of nowhere," Nathan said hesitantly into the silence, and the words spun through the air, "but I guess I'm hoping that at least part of the reason you've stayed as long as you have is not just because of the snow, but because of me." He paused, then added, "When we met on the road that day, when I first asked you to stay, you asked me a question—whether, when I woke up the next morning, I would want to believe it was real or wish I could pretend it was only a dream. The idea, the dream, of you meant something to me all those years ago, but you're not just an idea. You're here, and you're real. And I think I love you."

Angel drew back, away from him, and she saw hurt flash through Nathan's eyes.

"You can't love me," she said.

"Why not?" he asked, his words heavy.

So many thoughts flew through Angel's mind that she couldn't tell the beginning of one from the end of another. She tried to compose them all—the pain she had felt when Nathan had told her she would have to leave and walked out after learning of her pregnancy, the nagging feeling that he had proposed out of some irrational sense of duty, the misery of the months following her attack. "Everyone thinks that I'm broken and incomplete—that I've either sold or lost the most important piece of myself."

Nathan took one of her hands and looked intently into her eyes. "Because of what happened to you? That wasn't your fault. You know I don't think that."

Angel gently disentangled her hand from his. "I know," she said quietly, "but that doesn't make what happened less real. And even if the pieces are still there, I'm still trying to put them back together. You've only seen a few of them, and maybe you like what you've seen, but what about the pieces you haven't seen? I need someone who, when they look at me, sees more than brokenness. You couldn't even stay in the same room as me when I told you I was pregnant."

Nathan shook his head, staring at his freed hand like it had caught fire.

"Nathan," Angel said gently, "you couldn't even say you loved me —only that you thought you might. You have no business proposing marriage."

"I know people who have married for less," Nathan said, and from the expression on his face, Angel could tell that he knew it was the wrong thing to say as soon as the words left his mouth.

Still, she replied coolly, gritting her teeth against another spasm that rippled across her back and abdomen, "Yes, but I would prefer to marry for more."

They stared at each other across the table. Nathan was the first to fold. He stood abruptly, the legs of the chair scraping the floor. "Well then, I guess that's that. I'll give you a ride into town first thing tomorrow morning."

13

Even though Effie never knew my past, I couldn't forget what I did. I was reminded of it every time I saw her. I still stand by what I said—Effie jumped off that cliff all on her own, but I can't deny I gave her good reason to.

AT FIRST, Nathan wasn't sure what had awoken him. The room was silent for a moment, and then Angel cried out. In his half-awake state, Nathan nearly dismissed it as another of Angel's nightmares, but as she cried out again—a sound somewhere between a scream and a sob—he realized she was crying in pain.

Nathan didn't know how he got across the room. All he knew was that one instant he was sitting straight up in bed, and the next he was standing by the door.

"Angel, what is it? What's wrong?"

"The baby."

Nathan froze. Angel hadn't told him how far along she was, and he had been too preoccupied to ask. Still, he didn't have to ask to know it was early. Far too early.

"Can you get to the door?" Nathan asked.

"I don't think so." Angel's voice sounded strange—breathy and panting and sobbing.

Nathan hesitated. He knew how to bypass the lock—after all, he had made the door and latch himself. But he had never considered that he might have to force it open. In his mind, the lock was what had made their living arrangement acceptable.

Nathan's hesitation vanished as Angel cried again, a high keening sound. In one smooth motion, he lifted the pegs holding the door in place and then walked through the door.

Angel was kneeling beside the bed, knees splayed apart, face buried in her arms. She groaned as she turned her face toward him. Nathan quickly knelt beside her, raising a hand to her forehead. It was damp, sweaty. Cold.

"How long have you been like this?" Nathan asked.

"I don't know, a while," Angel answered.

"Why didn't you call me sooner?" Nathan asked, his voice tense.

Angel looked at him blankly. As Nathan looked at her eyes, he saw that they were seeing, and yet not. Disoriented.

"Not good, very not good," he muttered to himself, running his hand through his hair. "Never mind," he assured Angel as she looked at him, confused. At his words, she seemed to relax slightly. Noticing this, he spoke again, buying himself time to think. "You're going to be fine. Just keep breathing."

She needed a doctor. A midwife. Someone besides Nathan. There was no way she would make the trip into town. He would have to bring someone back.

Nathan stood as the thought gave him direction.

"Don't leave me," Angel begged, clinging to his hand.

Nathan hesitated, dropping back to his knees to meet her gaze. He took her face between his hands, searching it earnestly, wanting to find something more than the unsettling vagueness that had overpowered the usual brightness in her eyes. As he looked into her eyes though, Angel stared straight at him and yet beyond him, and a slow understanding crept over Nathan, kindling a new fear as he realized the dullness in Angel's eyes was due to more than her pain alone. It was a symptom of the slow ebbing of life. Nathan realized with a start that he was choosing between the possibility that if he left, Angel might die while he was gone, and the certainty that if he stayed, she would die in his arms.

There was no decision.

"I'm sorry," Nathan said, his voice breaking as he spoke. "I'll be back, I promise."

Please, he prayed, *please let me make it back in time.*

"DAVIS!" Nathan bellowed, his fist pounding frantically on the heavy door.

Nathan nearly struck the doctor as the door opened in midswing. The doctor froze, eyeing Nathan's fist, which had stopped inches from his face. Nathan slowly lowered his hand, and Ian Davis said, "What is it, Nathan? It's the middle of the night."

"It's Angel. She's . . . she's pregnant, but something is wrong and she's having the baby and I don't know exactly how far along she is but I know it's early."

Davis didn't speak, but Nathan read the doctor's expression. "It's not mine," Nathan said hotly, causing the doctor to smirk.

"But you wish it was." The doctor's statement was not a question, and Nathan's eyes narrowed. He placed a palm on the doorjamb, at the same height as Ian Davis's head, and leaned in closer.

"Don't push me, Davis," Nathan snarled.

The doctor averted his eyes. "I don't know, Nathan. It's not my place to be involved in this."

Nathan clenched his hands, gritting his teeth. "Involved in what? No. Never mind. That's not important right now. You are a doctor. How is it not your place?"

The doctor was silent. Nathan was growing more desperate with each second that passed.

"You owe me, Davis," he said quietly. The doctor raised his eyes to meet Nathan's. They were narrowed in understanding, but Nathan kept speaking, driving his words with a force he hoped would make the doctor hear them. "You owe me," he repeated, "for nine years ago when I got bucked off that 'horse.' But of course you know there was no horse. You knew my father beat me within an inch of my life, and you did nothing. Just a quick, 'Good luck, son,' and you were on your way."

The doctor's face flushed, and again he refused to meet Nathan's eyes.

"You owe me," Nathan repeated once more, quietly. Desperately.

"Well, I don't know about that," a soft female voice interrupted, "but this does seem to be a rather silly conversation. Of course, Ian will go, won't you, dear?"

Nelle had appeared.

The doctor's gaze flew to his wife.

Nelle looked at him solemnly. "My dear, I love you, but sometimes you worry far too much about the wrong things. You are, after all, a doctor, and what sort of doctor, when he is able, does not go when he is called?"

THE TRIP back to the cabin was at once a blur and painfully slow. Strange details stood out in Nathan's mind, like the way the moon-light filtered oddly down through the dwindling clouds and the last straggling snowflakes that seemed to appear out of midair. And yet, much like he couldn't remember crossing the room to Angel's door, he couldn't remember traveling back from town to the cabin.

He remembered the moment the cabin came into view, and pushing the cabin door open, and walking through the door to Angel's room, and meeting her eyes. Opening his mouth to speak, to reassure her.

And then the doctor pushed by Nathan, his initial reluctance to act now outweighed by sheer force of habit. The doctor motioned to Nathan, and together they lifted Angel from her position on the floor and laid her on the bed. Nathan's insides clenched as Angel cried out again. He found himself kneeling beside the bed, vaguely aware that Angel was holding his hand so tightly it hurt, and surprised she had the strength to do so.

The minutes dragged on like hours. In the back of his mind, Nathan knew he should have been exhausted, and yet he wasn't sure he could even blink. He felt like the anxiety was pumping through his veins. It was like the sharp, uncomfortable jolt of a tree branch giving way beneath him, except the feeling was constant. Every muscle in his body was tensed.

And then something changed. The doctor shifted, relaxed almost imperceptibly. Somehow, Angel seemed to know her work was almost done and, in spite of everything, seemed in control for the first time since Nathan had woken that night. Nathan held his breath.

Everything happened all at once. Angel cried out once more, and the baby came out. The doctor looked relieved, then troubled, and then there was silence. The baby did not cry.

As soon as the baby came out—limp and gray, with the cord wrapped around its neck—Nathan knew it was dead. The blow of that realization struck Nathan with more force than any that had been laid on him by his father's hand. A boy, Nathan saw. The baby had been a boy.

Nathan felt sick to his stomach, a sensation that worsened as he forced himself to meet Angel's eyes and he realized she already knew. Grief twisted her face, whitened with exhaustion and blood loss.

And the blood. There was so much blood.

ANGEL WAS FINALLY ASLEEP. The doctor turned to Nathan, and for once, Nathan knew he spoke with sincerity. "I'm sorry," he said.

Despite the doctor's earnestness, Nathan couldn't reply. There was nothing to say. So, he merely held out his hand. The doctor gripped Nathan's hand tightly, and they shook.

"Keep her warm," Ian instructed. "She's lost a lot of blood, but she should be okay. We're lucky I had the ergot to stop the bleeding—there's nothing I would have been able to do otherwise."

He hesitated, then added, "I am a coward at heart, Nathan. You knew that nine years ago. I wish I had come sooner to help Angel, right when you asked—"

"Would it have made a difference?" Nathan asked bluntly, too tired to be tactful.

There was a long pause, then the doctor answered, "No," and Nathan knew he spoke without guile. There was nothing more that could have been done.

Nathan nodded mutely, and after one last glance, the doctor released his hand and walked toward the door.

"Davis," Nathan said as the doctor reached the door, and he paused. "You did come, and I'm grateful for that."

Ian Davis met Nathan's eyes, then nodded. "Good luck, Nathan. To you and Angel both."

Then, he touched his hat and was gone.

The silence that followed was overwhelming. Nathan did not know what to do, and he found himself walking back and forth across the front room of the cabin. He was exhausted, but he didn't know whether he should sit with Angel, or leave her to rest, or sit with her while she rested.

It was his exhaustion that finally made the decision. Nathan lay in bed and fell asleep almost immediately, but his sleep was restless, filled with tossing and turning. When morning finally came, he grudgingly rolled out of bed, not feeling any more rested than he had when he had first lain down.

Nathan laid a piece of firewood on the coals left over from the night before. Sparks leapt from the burned wood as he scraped the cold ashes away. The new wood began smoking, the splinters nearest the hot coals darkening, and then a small flame licked its way out from underneath the kindling. Nathan glanced at Angel's door. It was open—the door still leaned against the wall where Nathan had set it after he had taken it down the night before.

Nathan hesitated, unsure whether he should leave Angel be or check on her, but as he hesitated, he heard a soft knock on the door. In his sleep-deprived state, Nathan foggily wondered whether the doctor had forgotten something, but when he opened the door, Olivia stood in front of him.

"How did you know?" Nathan asked, flabbergasted.

"Nelle," Olivia said simply.

Nathan stared at her, stunned. Never before in his life had he been so grateful to see Olivia.

"Is she awake?" Olivia asked.

Nathan shook his head mutely.

Olivia nodded, sitting down at the table as she did so. "You go about your business, Nathan," she said firmly. "I can take care of myself. I'll just wait here until she wakes up."

For a while, Nathan hovered in the front room, unsure of what to do and hoping Angel would wake. When she did not, and Olivia continued to sit silently at the table, Nathan finally gave up and left to milk the cow.

AS SOON AS NATHAN LEFT, Olivia rose from her spot at the table and walked to the doorless room.

"I know you're awake, dear," she said softly. "May I come in?"

Angel rolled over in bed to look at Olivia with red eyes and a tear-streaked face, then shrugged. She thought she should feel grateful that Olivia had come, but as hard as she tried, she could not bring herself to feel anything other than misery and overwhelming guilt. Angel mourned the loss of the tiny life that had grown inside her. It was a life she had never asked for, or wished for. One she had been terrified of. And yet she found herself grieving.

"It was my fault," she said to Olivia. There was no point in keeping the truth from her.

Olivia sat down beside Angel on the bed and took her hand. "How could it have possibly been your fault?"

"I didn't want the baby," Angel whispered. "When I started to wonder if I was pregnant, I hoped I was wrong, and when I knew it hadn't been a mistake—that I really was pregnant—I prayed it would go away. I screamed at God and asked him to take it away."

Olivia silently watched Angel as she began to sob. "And then I felt the baby move, and everything changed. I started wanting that baby, loving it. I would have fought for him to have a life that was good. And now he's gone."

Into the fog of Angel's mind came Olivia's voice. It sounded sad. "My dear, I don't believe it works that way. You will face enough sorrow. Do not add to it by blaming yourself."

Olivia sat with Angel until the flood of tears subsided, and then longer. It was Angel's words that finally broke the silence. "Would it still be possible for me to stay with you and Clark for a time?"

Olivia hesitated only for a moment before answering, "Of course you may. You are welcome to stay with us for as long as you wish."

Angel had faced the wall as she asked her question, but Olivia's hesitation made her move to face the other woman. As soon as she turned, she saw the reason for Olivia's hesitation. Nathan was standing in the doorway.

14

I *may have been a worse father to my own son than my father was to* *me, and that's saying something. I wanted him to be like me—if he* *turned out like me, I could believe none of this was my fault. But my* *son is nothing like me, even though I gave him every reason to be.*

EVEN THOUGH ANGEL had told him she could simply ride into town with Olivia, Nathan had insisted on taking Angel there, and Olivia had gone ahead to prepare a room for Angel. The trip had been largely silent, neither of them willing to make small talk, until they pulled up in front of Clark and Olivia's home.

"I hope you're not planning on leaving for good," Nathan said without looking at Angel, his eyes fixed somewhere between the ears of the horse in front of him.

Angel didn't reply. She couldn't bear to lie, and she couldn't bear to tell the truth, so she remained silent as she climbed down from the wagon. With a sudden burst of motion, Nathan tied the reins and hopped down from the seat of the wagon to stand beside Angel.

"I don't know what I did to make you feel like you have to leave," he said, taking her hand, "but I swear I'm going to try and find a way to make you believe you have a reason to stay."

Nathan's eyes held hers, and it wasn't until he released her hand that Angel realized she hadn't pulled away. Then, Nathan's certainty faded and he spoke pleadingly. "Just don't leave without saying goodbye."

Angel nodded mutely, and Nathan slowly climbed into the wagon, raised the reins, and clucked his tongue. The horses pulled forward. Angel stood outside the gate, watching until the wagon disappeared around a bend in the road and fighting the wrenching sensation inside her chest.

The grief she felt for the loss of her child was immutably linked with the hurt she had felt at Nathan's reaction to her pregnancy. No, it was more than that. Each emotion seemed to magnify the other, spiraling around each other until—even though she knew it did not make sense—a piece of her had begun to blame Nathan for the loss of the baby. A second, larger part of her shied away from sharing her grief with Nathan because she was afraid that her tribulation, her pain, was his salvation, his relief. The first part, the anger, she knew would fade. The second part, the fear, she was not so sure of.

When Angel finally turned to go inside, she found Olivia standing in the front doorway, watching. She gently guided Angel toward the spare bedroom. Clark raised an eyebrow as they passed the doorway into the sitting area, but Olivia shook her head, and he didn't speak. Only after Olivia had deposited Angel in the spare room did she speak, and when she did, she seemed to choose her words carefully. "How long will you be staying with us, dear?"

Angel shook her head miserably.

"What happened between you and Nathan?"

"Nothing," Angel answered. Nothing had ever happened between them, and nothing ever would.

Oliva considered Angel for a moment, obviously skeptical, but she did not press her. "Please make yourself at home. Take the time you need to settle in, and then come downstairs."

Olivia and Angel were just setting the table for supper when

Clark walked in, carrying a letter and looking upset. Olivia stood, fear in her eyes. "What is it? Is it about Felicity?"

Clark shook his head. "No, but I'm not sure this news is much better." He gave a slight wave of the letter. "Will Pratchet down south of the Platte just sent me an urgent message to let me know he thought he saw James leaving the saloon there in town. He wasn't sure, but you know that horse James had—the paint—it's hard to mistake. So unless the horse has found its way to a new owner . . ." Clark trailed off, then continued. "Pratchet reckons James is making his way back here, although he seems to be taking his time about it."

Olivia paled. "Do you think he knows where Felicity is?"

Clark shook his head. "I can't see how he would. We didn't tell anyone where she was going to be teaching. Besides, he hasn't seen her in years. Even if they crossed paths it's not likely he would recognize her."

Olivia seemed to relax slightly, then spoke, her voice tight. "Why would he chance coming back when he's suspected of murder?"

Clark shrugged, and his eyes were tired as he responded, "Even if he did kill that man, James is smart enough to know that if he lies low for a while—long enough for the initial anger to die down—he's safe. No one saw him kill the man. There's no proof, and no one's going to convict him."

THE DAYS of the week blurred together, and Angel soon found herself in the midst of yet another Sunday, sitting uncomfortably on the front pew in between Nathan and Olivia. Despite Angel's nearly constant silence toward everyone and her always constant lack of expression toward him, Nathan had persisted in visiting her in town nearly every day since he had left her at Clark and Olivia's house. He never pressed her to speak, merely sat—usually in silence himself—with Angel, and Clark, and Olivia in the quiet moments of the evening before returning to the homestead to take care of the evening chores.

Angel couldn't deny that a part of her was glad to see him. She felt less unsettled when Nathan was around. He gave Angel something to ground herself to—a constant in the midst of emotions and thoughts that constantly swirled through her mind despite her best efforts to push them away.

But another part of her—the part that always won—struggled with the piercing pain Nathan's presence brought. Pain was a constant. Depending on how recently she had sobbed out her emotions, Angel's grief alternated between an overwhelming sense of loss, and a hollow, empty numbness she was afraid would never leave. So it wasn't the pain that bothered her.

No, it was the fact that Nathan, simply by being there, reminded Angel over and over and over again how he had walked out the door after she had told him of her pregnancy. It didn't matter that he had come back—Angel couldn't shake the fear that he had done so because he had felt obligated to do so, rather than because he had resolved the thing that had caused him to walk away in the first place. Nathan himself had admitted that he had left because he hadn't known—and still didn't know—how to deal with her pregnancy.

And now . . . now the baby was gone. It was so easy, Angel thought, for Nathan to say all the right things now that the baby was gone. But it was so hard for her to trust his words. She knew he meant the words he spoke, and yet, she couldn't help wondering if Nathan would have spoken the same words if she hadn't lost the baby. Now, every time Nathan spoke to her, Angel found herself nearly staring through him, a fact she knew was not lost on Nathan.

She had heard Olivia whispering to Nathan, "Just give her time," and had almost wanted to laugh. Time for what? To heal from a wound Angel knew would always exist? To forget Nathan had walked away? Or perhaps Olivia meant time to change the past. All three options seemed equally impossible to Angel.

As Clark began to speak, Angel was jerked from her own thoughts, enough for her to hear another, female voice mutter. The words were loud enough to carry across the congregation, but soft enough that she almost believed she hadn't been meant to hear.

"It's not right that it should be buried in the church graveyard, next to good, God-fearing people. That baby was an abomination, the child of a harlot. Its death was God's judgment."

Angel froze, her entire body growing cold as fury spread silently through her body. Her shock held her motionless. All except for her hands. Her hands trembled, and she stared at them in awe, vaguely wondering at the barely contained anger that held her prisoner, yet made parts of her frame respond in such an uncontrollable manner.

And then, the tension in her body snapped. If they wanted her reaction, they would have it. She would stand. She would speak. She would scream.

With a sudden burst of motion, Angel stood, then turned to face the sea of faces. One face—Valentine's—stood out, gazing at Angel with contempt, and Angel wondered if it was Valentine's voice that had carried across the congregation. Angel opened her mouth to speak, then paused as the eyes that had stared at her when she had first stood drifted upward, as one, to focus on a point somewhere behind her. Nathan tugged at her hand, then motioned for her to turn, and Angel slowly faced the front of the room, glancing at Nathan as she did so.

But Nathan was no longer looking at her. Eyes narrowed and lips parted, Nathan was staring at Clark with an intensity Angel had not seen before. It was as though he had never seen Clark before. As Angel followed Nathan's gaze and rested her own on Clark, she understood Nathan's strange expression, and she stopped trying to tug her hand free. The strength radiating from Clark commanded the attention of every person in the room, and the silence the mutinous whisper had carried over had nothing on the stillness that filled the room in the moments before Clark began to speak.

When he did speak, it was a voice of quietness, of calm, of unarguable strength.

"This woman is no harlot," he said, gesturing toward Angel, "and her child—her son—was no abomination. He was loved. Not only by his mother, but by that same God whom you profess to love.

"I suggest we all take some time to ponder the nature of that God whom we claim to follow. The funeral will take place as planned. Any who disagree with this decision are welcome to remain absent."

As Clark fell silent, Angel held her breath, waiting. Whispers flooded the room, and then came the sound Angel was dreading. The outraged mutters, the creak of pews as people stood, the hollow sound of shoes on the wooden floor.

And yet, the roar of noise Angel had expected did not come. She tentatively turned to look behind herself and saw only a handful of people indignantly leaving. Once she noticed this, she began scanning the faces of those who remained. Most determinedly faced forward, eyes fixed on Clark or on the floor, but a few quietly met her gaze.

"Now," Clark said quietly after the last person had passed through the church doors and Angel had sat back down, "I would like to begin our sermon for today."

Angel didn't hear the words Clark spoke after that. She was still too stunned to think of anything other than the events that had just transpired. She snuck a glance at Nathan. He seemed to be confused, fighting some internal battle. Angel glanced at Clark. His words were for the congregation as a whole, but for a moment he had looked at Olivia while he spoke. Angel turned her gaze toward Olivia. She was smiling faintly in Clark's direction with something like pride.

ANGEL STARED DETERMINEDLY at the ground as people gathered for the funeral. Partially, she was absorbed in her own thoughts, and partially, she didn't want to be forced to acknowledge the small numbers of people in attendance. Then, Nathan nudged her, and she looked up.

She was surrounded by people. People who had arrived quietly and without her notice. People with bowed heads. People who shared in her sorrow, even though she scarcely knew them, and they hardly knew her. There was even a little girl holding a wreath woven of boughs from a fir tree.

Angel felt tears of gratitude swell up in her eyes She blinked, stubbornly refusing to let them fall. But as hard as she tried, Angel could not keep the tears from trailing down her face when the tiny coffin was lowered into the ground. The tears came and went on the silent journey back to Clark and Olivia's home. Even so, during one quiet moment, she found her heart lightened by the memory of a little girl placing a homemade wreath on the coffin.

MORE THAN ANYTHING, Nathan wanted to be able to take Angel in his arms—to hold her close and comfort her when she started to cry—but he knew the gesture was not one Angel would welcome, so instead, he clasped his hands together to stop himself from reaching out to her.

On the way from the cabin to Clark and Olivia's house, Nathan had asked Angel point-blank, "If I told you I loved you, would you stay?"

Angel had been silent for a long moment before answering, and then when she had answered, she had responded with even greater bluntness than he had anticipated. "No, I would not. And it's not because I don't care for you, because I do. It's because of how you reacted when you found out I was pregnant."

"I was caught off guard—" Nathan had protested, but Angel cut him off.

"No, Nathan. You were upset that I was pregnant."

"I was upset because I knew how people would react," Nathan had said quietly.

"That is the problem," Angel responded. "You keep telling me you were worried about how people would react, but when I told you I was pregnant, it was because for the first time since I've been here I didn't care what anyone else would say. You were the only one whose reaction I cared about, and I finally wasn't scared to tell you the whole truth. I finally hoped you might prove me wrong—that Olivia might be right—but you reacted exactly the way I'd been afraid you would all along. You told me I would have to leave. And now, the baby is gone, and you want to say you love me.

"I know you believe your words are sincere, but I don't believe you would have spoken the same words if I was still pregnant."

"Is there anything I can say to change your mind?" Nathan had asked quietly.

Angel had shaken her head. "I don't know."

Now, Angel's words echoed over and over in Nathan's mind as he stood beside her, watching tears stream down her face, but unable to do anything to comfort her. An uncomfortable knowledge slowly began to creep over him, and Nathan realized that the outward vulnerability Angel was showing had in no way diminished the emotional wall she had thrown up between herself and Nathan. He didn't know if he would ever find the words to change her mind, but in that moment he realized he didn't care. He only wanted her to trust him enough, again, to let him be there.

15

I hate them all. Every time I see them, they remind me of the worst mistakes I've made.

∽

ANGEL WAS BROWSING the goods at the general store—Olivia had asked her to go to the store and purchase a pound of flour—when a female voice interrupted her thoughts.

"Can I help you, dear?"

The tone of the woman's voice plainly conveyed that the term of endearment was anything but, and the hair on the back of Angel's neck prickled as she slowly turned to face her assailant. The daughter of Carl, the man who owned the general store. Valentine.

Angel kept her tone even as she replied, "Yes, please. I'd like a pound of flour."

Valentine turned, walking toward the counter, and Angel followed. As Valentine weighed the flour, she spoke casually, almost sounding friendly. "I hear you are staying with Nathan's aunt and uncle now."

"Yes."

"Such an odd living arrangement that was—you staying with Nathan."

Angel remained silent. It seemed to take Valentine forever to measure the flour as she continued. "Remind me how you came to be staying with him?"

"That would be difficult to do," Angel answered, "seeing as how I can't recall ever giving you a reason in the first place."

Valentine's eyes narrowed. "A person who avoids answering questions usually has something to hide."

Angel gritted her teeth, torn between a desire to defend herself and resentment that Valentine—and nearly everyone else—seemed to feel entitled to whatever defense Angel could provide. Angel was so tired of arguing. It seemed the only reason most people questioned her was to create an opportunity for themselves to tell her why she was wrong—that her attack really had been her fault, that her living situation with Nathan really had been improper, that she was just too flawed to realize these things for herself. The last thing Angel wanted to do was argue with Valentine because she knew it was the same argument she'd had many times over, and it was argument she could only ever lose. Still, Angel found herself answering Valentine's questions, the words leaving Angel's mouth almost without her bidding.

"He was helping me."

Valentine sniffed. "I'm sure. Perhaps you were 'helping' Nathan as well."

Angel seethed, fighting to keep her voice even. "Not in the way you imply."

"Hmm," Valentine answered, not bothering to hide her disbelief. "Why did you leave?" She smirked, pushing the bag of flour across the counter to Angel. "Perhaps Nathan tired of your 'help'?"

Angel accepted the flour, holding Valentine's gaze as she did so. Valentine was the first to look away, but as Angel turned to leave, Valentine said, "You may have been an interesting diversion, but Nathan can do better."

"Like you?" Angel asked with a raised eyebrow.

Valentine glanced around the store, making sure no one else was in earshot before answering, "Yes. But don't tell Daddy." She smirked, then added, "Not that he would believe you anyway, but it would upset him dreadfully to hear such rumors about his daughter."

"If the rumors of your interest in Nathan would be so dreadful, why would you even suggest such a thing?"

"Just because Daddy doesn't see Nathan's attributes doesn't mean that I am blind to them."

Angel gave a snort of disgust, and disbelief colored her voice as she said, "And you think Nathan would be interested in you?"

Valentine leaned forward, suddenly uncomfortably close even with the counter between herself and Angel. "This is my town," Valentine hissed. "You would do well to remember you are merely a guest, and an unwelcome one at that."

Just then the bell on the door jingled, and Nathan walked through the door. Both Valentine and Angel gaped at him for a moment, and then Valentine returned her attention to Angel, smiling sweetly. "You should probably go, dear. I know it must be terribly awkward to be in the same room as Nathan now that you are no longer . . . sharing one with him."

Angel gave Valentine a flat look, then turned to nod a greeting at Nathan. Valentine tilted her head to the side and looked up at Nathan through her eyelashes.

"Hello, Nathan," she simpered.

Nathan returned Valentine's greeting with a brief nod, scarcely acknowledging her, then waved warmly at Angel.

"Perhaps I will see you later?" Nathan asked as Angel passed by him on the way to the door.

Angel hesitated for just a moment, then returned his smile. "Perhaps. I am on my way back to Clark and Olivia's, so if you visit them before you leave town, I will likely be there."

Nathan grinned. "I will stop by later then."

The chill breeze struck Angel as she exited the general store. Warmer weather was showing signs of being just around the corner, but it hadn't yet made its appearance. As she strolled down the street, Angel closed her eyes and breathed in the smell of approaching spring—of melting ice and overcast days, of mud and the promise of new life.

Angel paused midstride as she walked down the street. She could feel it in the back of her nose—not a scent, but the barest memory of one. Her skin started to prickle almost before she began to place the memory. And then the breeze twirled around her, bringing with it the faint smell of stale smoke and alcohol and shaving soap.

Her breaths grew shallow, quiet. She stood motionless, even though every muscle in her body was tensed and the only thought in her mind was screaming to run. Finally, when the silence dragged on and the scent did not fade from her nostrils, she moved, turning slowly to face in the direction she had come.

At first she didn't see him. There were a few people scattered on the street—a man speaking with the blacksmith about his horse's loose shoe, two women visiting and holding cloth-covered baskets, another man letting his horse drink from the watering trough. Then a gravelly voice spoke from underneath the shaded overhang of the saloon. "Hello again, Angel-no-more."

Angel froze in her search, still not looking directly at the man. She didn't want to see him, didn't want to face that voice again. As footsteps came closer though, she forced herself to turn and look.

Nathan.

And yet . . . it was not.

The height, the build, the angles of the face, the dark eyes. They were all the same, but it was a different sort of sameness, like how the color of new grass and the color of a sick sky were both indisputably green and yet so indisputably different. The contrast between the man's cleanly shaven face and his otherwise slovenly appearance struck her once again. Again—and it truly was again, for now she could remember, and she couldn't believe she could ever have forgotten.

The man stood deliberately and uncomfortably close to her, yet far enough away that Angel would not be able to step away without giving offense. Should she be afraid to offend him, to make him angry? Should she scream? The man watched her without expression. Finally, she spoke—and now she knew his name, for there was only one person he could be. "Hello again, James."

James eyed her, and a slow, lazy smile spread across his face. His words were slightly slurred as he said, "I was worried there for a minute that you'd gone and forgot me. But you haven't forgotten— you've gone and learned my name."

"Does that bother you?" Angel asked coolly.

James laughed. "Nah. In fact, I wish you'd known it before. Maybe you could have screamed it when—"

Angel slapped him, cutting him off, and his slurred words turned into a snarl as he caught her wrist in his much larger hand. He pulled her in closer to him, and she looked frantically to the sides. The smell of worn-out smoke and liquor stung her nose, and she gagged. James looked down at her in disgust. He pushed her away, holding her at arm's length, considering her. His grip didn't slacken.

And then Nathan was there. "Let her go."

James's expression turned sour, but he managed to smile as he released Angel and pushed her toward Nathan. Nathan caught her as she stumbled from the sudden force, and he held her shoulders with both hands to steady her. He held her for only a moment longer than necessary. A moment longer than he would have steadied a stranger on the street. A moment long enough for James's eyes to narrow.

Nathan seemed to realize his hesitation had drawn James's attention, and he pulled his hands away from Angel as though they'd been burned. James looked back and forth from Angel to Nathan. Then, his eyes widened and he slowly nodded to himself. Ignoring Nathan, he looked at Angel and asked, "Does he know?"

Angel didn't answer.

"Know what?" Nathan asked.

Angel felt a flush creep into her cheeks, and James spoke with incredulous delight. "He doesn't know, does he?" James laughed, almost to himself.

"What don't I know?" Nathan repeated, his voice rising.

"Nothin'," James said. "You don't know nothin'."

James stepped backward away from them, raising a hand to the brim of his hat in mock salute. "Nathan, Angel."

His salute was a dismissal, and he turned and walked away.

16

My brother wanted to shoot me today. I saw it in his eyes. But he couldn't, and I know the real reason why. It had nothing to do with his so-called principles against harming an unarmed man, or even the fact that I saved his life so long ago. It was because he blames himself for the way I am.

NATHAN HAD to force himself to remain where he stood and not follow after his father. If Angel hadn't been standing beside him, white as though she'd seen a ghost—or maybe as though she herself was the ghost—Nathan wasn't sure that he would have been able to remain in place.

He cast a sideways glance at Angel. "Did my father hurt you?"

Angel looked at him sharply, seeming to weigh her words before she answered. "I am fine."

"Let me at least walk with you back to Clark and Olivia's."

Angel shook her head. "There's no need. I am—"

Nathan cut her off. "I know you're fine. You already said that, but I want to make sure it stays that way."

As they walked, Nathan glanced at Angel from time to time. She looked stricken. Nathan thought she looked even more miserable than he himself felt. But then, he had had years to grow accustomed to his father. Angel had not.

When Nathan and Angel arrived at Clark and Olivia's house, Nathan paused before opening the gate, eyeing Angel. She had not spoken a word since Nathan had insisted on walking her back to the house.

"Are you going to be all right?" he asked with concern.

Angel nodded, but avoided his eyes as she answered, "I'll be fine."

"I'm sorry I can't stay to visit you, and Clark, and Olivia. Now that I know my father's in town, there are a few things I need to take care of on the farm—the land deed is there, and I need to make sure my father doesn't find it. I'll be back tomorrow.

"If you stay with Clark and Olivia, you should be safe enough. My father will likely come after me before he causes trouble anywhere else."

"If he does come after you, will you be able to handle him alone?" Angel asked.

There was no doubt in Nathan's voice as he answered, "Yes."

For a moment, Angel hesitated as though she wanted to say something more, but at the last second she slipped around Nathan and through the gate, closing it between them.

"Goodbye, Nathan."

Surprised by Angel's abruptness, Nathan nodded a farewell. He barely had time to raise his hand to the brim of his hat before Angel walked into the house and shut the door behind herself.

Nathan placed a hand on top of the gate and let out a long breath. Even though Angel had recently begun occasionally speaking to Nathan without his directly addressing her, the distance between them didn't seem to be diminishing. If anything, it was solidifying, and Nathan knew that once that window closed, there would be no opening it again.

OF COURSE NATHAN *didn't know*, Angel had wanted to scream at James. How could he? Angel had only just realized the truth herself.

Angel thought back to that day at the saloon. She tried to remember coming down the stairs, the shouts and voices she must have heard as her uncle and his assailant argued. And she did remember, but no more clearly than before. Everything in the minutes before she had hit her head was fuzzy, pieced together haphazardly. She closed her eyes, trying to picture a face, then froze as her imagination filled in the holes in her memory with Nathan's image. Angel pushed the vision away, but the image of Nathan—a Nathan with darker, emptier eyes—lingered, and the words, "I am my father's son," echoed over and over in her mind. She shuddered again.

No, Nathan did not know his father had been the father of Angel's child, and she wanted to keep it that way.

But when she opened the door to Clark and Olivia's home, Angel was immediately met by Olivia, who looked up from a sock she was darning.

"You're back sooner than I expected. Did you meet Nathan?"

"Yes," Angel answered, still walking.

Olivia set down her needlework. "Angel?"

Angel stopped but did not turn. "Yes?"

"What happened?"

Angel didn't answer immediately. For once, she knew exactly the words to explain what had happened—her already tumultuous world had been upended yet again, her humiliation compounded, her misery renewed—but that did not mean she wanted to speak them. Olivia remained silent, seeming to know that if she waited long enough, patiently enough, eventually Angel would speak.

And even though Angel knew what Olivia was doing, she found herself complying. Slowly turning to face Olivia, Angel answered, her voice sounding hoarse even to her own ears. "It was James," she whispered.

Confusion flooded over Olivia's face. "James is back?" she asked.

Angel shook her head, her whisper dropping even lower. "No.

Well, yes." Olivia's eyes widened but Angel continued. "But it's not that. The baby. James was the father.'"

"Oh," Olivia said slowly. Then, "Oh!" Her face paled and her eyes widened in understanding.

Angel watched a myriad of expressions and questions fly over Olivia's face. "Does Nathan know?" Olivia asked.

Angel shook her head mutely.

"I see," Olivia said softly.

Angel glanced at her sharply. It wasn't that she didn't trust Olivia—she did. But she didn't believe Olivia would have any reservations about passing along to Nathan—or Clark—the information Angel had just shared. "You can't tell him," Angel said sharply.

Olivia regarded her sadly. "The idea was not in my thoughts, my dear, and I won't tell Nathan. But I think that you should." She held up a hand as Angel opened her mouth to protest. "When you are ready."

Olivia's next words were so soft Angel barely heard them. "But I hope for both your sakes, that comes sooner than later."

Angel stared at Olivia. "How can you say that? I've told you how Nathan reacted when I told him I was pregnant." She covered her face with her hands and sat down on the edge of the bed. "I can't bear to think of what he would say if he found out the baby was his father's."

Olivia was silent for a moment, then said, "I don't understand everything that has happened with you and Nathan. I know that he hurt you deeply. I also know that he cares for you deeply. I cannot tell you what you should do, because I am not entirely sure what is wrong, but I can tell you that you need to decide whether you believe it can be fixed."

"And if I don't think it can?" Angel asked.

Olivia was silent for a moment, then said, "My dear, forgive me if I speak too honestly, but if you don't believe that what is broken with you and Nathan can be fixed, then the question you need to ask yourself is why you are still here."

"James is back in town," Clark said darkly.

"Yes, I heard," Olivia said. "Angel and Nathan already had the misfortune of encountering him on the street this morning."

Clark's head jerked up. "He didn't cause any trouble, did he? It was broad daylight."

When Angel said nothing, Olivia spoke dryly in her place, "Has that ever deterred James?"

Clark inclined his head slightly in acknowledgement.

"Was he always that way, Nathan's father?" Angel asked.

Olivia looked surprised by Angel's question—Angel herself was unsure what had prompted her to ask it—then turned to Clark with raised eyebrows, plainly deferring Angel's question to him. Clark held Olivia's eyes for a moment, having a silent conversation Angel was not privy to. When he spoke, it was only a few words.

"James was never that good. But he wasn't always so bad."

Clark appeared to hope that would be enough explanation, but as Angel waited in silence, he glanced at Olivia as though asking permission. When Olivia merely shrugged half-heartedly, Clark sighed and shook his head in resignation.

"Our father was a lot like James in many ways. He had a mean streak, but he hid it real well. James, well, he used to hide it well—he could be real charming."

"Our father died when James was nineteen and I was just turned eighteen. The day of the funeral, everyone was all in a tizzy because James never showed up. 'What kind of son doesn't show up for his own father's funeral?' people asked. But I knew he was there. After everyone else left, he came out and just stood there, looking at the mound of dirt where our father had been buried. And then he kind of just laughed. He started to walk away, but then he stopped and turned and spit on the grave. And then he left. He never saw me.

"James was impulsive and jealous and vindictive—the kind to get offended easily. It was easy for him to justify just about anything if he thought someone had done—or was going to do—him wrong. When he drank, the alcohol made every bad part of him worse. He was good at hiding it though. You couldn't tell when he'd been drinking unless something set him off.

"I remember one time James confronted me. He was convinced I was seeing Olivia behind his back—"

Olivia's eyes widened, and she frantically shook her head with a minuscule motion. Clearly, Clark had said something she had not anticipated in his explanation to Angel. Clark cut himself off abruptly, but it was too late. The final piece had been laid out, and Angel's lips parted with a sharp intake of breath as the puzzle came together before her eyes.

The boy Olivia had been engaged to before she married Clark. It had been Nathan's father.

Angel felt sick. When Olivia had told Angel the story, it had been awful. Now, it was so much worse. In her story, Olivia had said there were two boys, but she had never said they were brothers—an omission that had probably been deliberate. Angel clenched her hands, digging her fingernails into her palms as understanding washed over her.

Clark had watched his brother pursue the woman he loved. He had watched her fall in love with his brother, watched her become engaged to him. Despite reservations, he had let them be, hoping for their happiness, for Olivia's happiness. He had even planned to leave early for his education with the hope James would let go of his belief that Clark was seeing Olivia behind his back. And then, on the evening before Clark left for college, he had gone to say goodbye to Olivia, and he had found her how James left her—crying on the porch.

It hadn't taken him long to realize what had happened. James—impulsive, jealous, and vindictive—had taken his anger out on Olivia. When she had seen how angry Clark was, Olivia had begged him not to go after James. Clark had succumbed to Olivia's pleading that no one else know, and James had been left to his own.

Olivia hadn't told Angel the rest of the story, but it was easy for Angel to fill in. When Olivia found out she was pregnant, she would have told only one person. The only person who knew what James had done, and the only person she could tell. Clark.

Clark had proposed to Olivia, who had accepted. Their wedding had been rushed, and unexpected to everyone. It would have been easy for James to start the rumors that Olivia had been unfaithful to him with his brother—why else would she be marrying Clark, instead of him, and so quickly at that?

No wonder Clark hated James.

17

For a long time, maybe even up until this moment, I blamed him too. But the fact is, I've been stone-cold sober for a week now, and things don't always look the same on the other side of the bottle.

"You didn't tell me." Angel spoke the obvious. She couldn't bring herself to feel anger, or even surprise, that Olivia had kept this secret to herself. She suspected Olivia's reasons for silence closely resembled her own.

Olivia watched her warily, as though expecting her to lash out. Instead Angel merely shook her head and asked dully, "Does Clark know? Did you tell him about my . . . encounter . . . with James?"

Clark jerked his head around to stare at Angel.

Olivia hesitated and then spoke with reproach. "No. I did not feel it was my place to share that information."

"What information?" Clark growled.

Olivia glanced at Angel, but when Angel remained silent, Olivia spoke, choosing her words carefully, delicately. Lightly. "It seems, dear, that Angel and I unfortunately have more in common with one another than we originally thought." Her eyes hardened slightly, and Clark's eyes narrowed as she continued. "Namely, James, and what he took from both of us."

Angel knew Clark could not have mistook Olivia's meaning, but he said nothing. And as he said nothing, his eyes grew harder and harder. His jaw clenched, and his breathing grew heavy. The tips of his fingers pressed into the wood of the table with such force they turned white. Then, slowly, deliberately, he stood. One hand rested at his side. The other, he flexed over and over. Angel could hear one knuckle pop each time his fingers curled together to meet his palm.

Angel took her cue from Olivia and stood silently and uncomfortably as Clark obviously struggled to calm himself. Gradually, the deep red faded from the back of his neck, and his breathing quieted. When he turned around, his jaw was still clenched.

"I know I promised you I wouldn't go after James, years ago . . ." Clark's words to Olivia drew Angel back to the conversation. "But I don't know if I can keep that promise anymore." His voice shook, and Olivia took his hand.

"You know why I asked that promise of you," Olivia said.

Clark's face twisted, and he turned from Olivia as he said, "I know you don't want anyone to know what happened to you. I know that unless others know what he did, it will look like I killed my brother for no reason at all, and I could be hung for that. I know you wouldn't let that happen—you'd tell the world the truth before you'd see me hanged. And I know you'd never forgive me for putting you in a situation where you had to make that choice." Clark paused, then continued. "But I don't know it'd be possible for me to be a man and keep living knowing I allowed him to go on the way he is after all he's done."

Then, refusing to meet Olivia's eyes, he turned and walked out the door.

Angel opened her mouth to speak and Olivia shook her head. "Leave it be. Clark will back after he's thought on all this a while. For now, let's clean up after dinner."

As they cleaned the dishes, Angel ventured a question. "Has Clark ever raised his voice to you?"

Olivia smiled. "No, although I'm sure there's been times he had the chance."

Angel thought for a moment before asking, "And you? Have you ever argued with him at all?"

Olivia laughed. The sound was strange to Angel after the conversation that had come only minutes before. "Oh heavens, yes. We argue all the time. But he never raises his voice, and I don't think I could have the heart to raise mine knowing he would never do the same."

Angel felt perplexity color her expression as she pondered Olivia's words and her memories of the saloon. "I'm not sure I've ever met anyone else who thought that way," she admitted as she wiped a dish and placed it in its holding place.

Olivia smiled, then said, "I've never met anyone else like Clark."

They worked in silence for a several minutes, and then Olivia added, "By the way, Nathan will be joining us for dinner tomorrow."

"Oh?" Angel asked, her voice carefully even, as it always was when Olivia mentioned Nathan.

Without looking up from the dish she was drying, Olivia asked, "Have you given any thought to what I said the other day?"

Angel grimaced. "I would prefer not to speak of it."

Olivia's expression plainly indicated that she did not care one whit whether or not Angel preferred to speak of it, and she opened her mouth to say so, but Angel cut her off with a raised hand. "But I am a guest in your home, and as such, I do owe you some explanation, so I will give you that."

Olivia's expression softened. "I do hope, my dear, that you understand I ask with dual motivations. I ask both as Nathan's aunt and, I hope, as your friend."

Angel nodded, feeling some of her defensiveness fade. Instead of answering Olivia's question immediately, however, she asked one of her own. "How did Clark react when you told him you were pregnant?"

Olivia shot Angel a sideways glance. "He wasn't happy. I'm sure you're not surprised to hear that."

Angel shook her head, and Olivia continued. "I had to talk him down from going after James all over again. I think he was angrier at me for not wanting him to go after James than anything else. He thought I was defending James. He was going to go after James, even after I begged him not to. I was so afraid someone else would find out what happened I started crying, and I think that's what finally made Clark realize that none of my pleading was about James.

"He promised me he wouldn't go after James and then he asked me to marry him."

Angel made a face. "Poor timing seems to run in the family."

And she told Olivia of Nathan's reaction when he had learned of her pregnancy and how he had walked out of the cabin. She told Olivia of the men who had come to the cabin while Nathan was gone and of the words Nathan had spoken to them—*I am my father's son*. And she told Olivia what Nathan had spoken to her after the men had left, of his proposal, and of his declaration of uncertain love.

Olivia listened in attentive silence, and when Angel finally stopped speaking, she said sadly, "Oh, Nathan."

"I don't know what to think. And I'm afraid of what Nathan thinks. Of what he will think," Angel said helplessly.

Olivia looked at her intently. "You will never know unless you talk to him." She raised a hand, cutting off Angel's protest as she opened her mouth to speak. "I know some of what Nathan said to you was poorly thought out. Nathan does not have his father's way with words —something you should be grateful for. I learned long ago to beware the charmer who knows he is charming.

"It is true that if you talk to Nathan, there is the possibility that he will confirm your fears to be true. But personally, I believe you should have a little more faith in Nathan."

Angel thought for a moment, her eyes distant. "Tell me, who does Nathan take after more—Clark or James?"

Olivia laughed without humor, then answered, "That is an easy question to answer. Whenever I look at Nathan, I can see James. Not just in his looks, but in his mannerisms, his voice, his bearing and stubbornness. Nathan has much of James in him—" Angel stiffened, and Olivia continued gently. "But Nathan is different from James in the ways that count, and perhaps more importantly, he has a strong desire to be nothing like him. Nathan has James's temper and impulsiveness, but he also has control over himself in a way that James never did. Nathan has the ability to forgive, and to admit he is wrong when he needs to, which is something James was never able to do. Nathan is good in a way I don't believe James ever was."

Angel nodded, then exhaled sharply, her mouth twisting as she considered Olivia's words.

At that moment, Clark stalked back into the house, and as one, Olivia and Angel looked up at him. Avoiding both their eyes, Clark strode to the edge of the table, where he stood for a time, drumming his fingers against the wood. When he finally spoke, his voice was heavy, but he spoke the words without hesitation.

"I am sorry for what I am about to ask you, Angel, as I am sure you have little desire to relive these memories, but I must know the circumstances surrounding your encounter—how long ago, where you were at the time, and the like—with James."

Angel nodded slowly, her stomach clenching. "It was about seven months ago."

Clark's eyes narrowed as though she had confirmed his suspicion, but when he said nothing, Angel continued. "I was living with my uncle at his saloon in Oklada—"

"You uncle didn't, by any chance, go by the name of Thomas Bernard, did he?" Clark interrupted Angel, speaking with quiet intensity.

"Well, he went by Tom, but Thomas Bernard was his given name, yes." Angel nodded.

Clark began pacing rapidly back and forth in the small room. "No real witnesses . . . only an empty-headed girl who couldn't—or wouldn't—describe her attacker . . ." Clark spoke softly out loud, as though repeating someone else's words. Mortified, Angel felt her cheeks redden at his words.

"Clark," Olivia chided him sharply, and Clark shook his head, but before he could reply, Angel spoke urgently, her voice shaking.

"I didn't know until today it was him. I couldn't remember. But then while I was walking through town I saw him, and I heard his voice, and the things he said—"

"You don't have to explain yourself to me," Clark interrupted her gently. "And I'm sorry, Angel. I didn't mean to imply—of course I don't believe what I said just now. I was only repeating aloud the speculation I had heard about the event at the time. Everything people said at the time, how little anyone knew about what had happened . . . It makes more sense now."

Looking directly at Angel, he said, "You must testify against James."

Angel paled. Where she had felt her cheeks flush with color only moments before, she now felt the heat drain out of her face to be replaced with ice, her heart pounding. "I will not."

Clark sat beside her, his expression almost pleading. "There is no one else who witnessed what he did—you are the only one who saw him kill that man—"

Angel interrupted him firmly. "My uncle."

Clark's expression softened. "Yes, you are the only one who knows James killed your uncle."

"What will he do if I speak against him? What if they don't listen to me? What if they let him go?" Angel asked the questions as they ran through her mind, her voice small and panicked.

"The evidence was always against James. There are men who saw James at the saloon the night before, who said he'd been drinking and that he got into a nasty fight with the owner and got himself thrown out. But without a witness to the murder, nothing ever stuck. You are that witness, Angel. If you testify, even James won't be able to talk his way out of the facts, and if he can't do that, he won't be able to hurt you."

"I can't tell Nathan it was his father," Angel whispered.

Clark watched her, his face unreadable. "If you cannot speak against James, he will always stand between you and Nathan—whether Nathan knows the truth or not."

As soon as Nathan arrived at Clark and Olivia's house the next day, he could tell something was wrong—more wrong even than it should have been with James's return. Clark answered the door, his face tense. When he saw it was Nathan, his face relaxed, but he looked over Nathan's shoulder as he pulled the door closed.

Olivia barely paused in her pacing to acknowledge Nathan's entrance. When Nathan glanced inquiringly at Clark, he merely shook his head, then said, "I spoke to the sheriff this morning. They're looking for James. As you can probably imagine, Olivia is—we are—on edge."

Nathan shook his head. "I don't understand. Why are they looking for my father now? Has he done something else?"

Clark paused, eyeing Nathan. "No. But the man your father was accused of killing last spring—a witness has been located."

Nathan narrowed his eyes. "A witness? Now? Why didn't he come forward before?"

At Nathan's words, both Clark and Olivia suddenly stilled. Olivia glanced at Clark, then said, "I believe she—the witness—was afraid of retaliation. And I don't think she was able to identify James as the killer until now."

"She?" Nathan asked. "The witness is a girl?"

Olivia and Clark glanced at each other again. "Yes."

Then, looking around, Nathan suddenly noticed who was missing from the room. "Where's Angel?" he asked.

Her face pinched, Olivia answered, "We're not sure. Clark left early this morning to fetch the sheriff, and when I woke this morning, she was already gone."

The pit of Nathan's stomach dropped. "And my father is still out there?"

Clark and Olivia's silence was answer enough, and Nathan turned and ran out the door.

As soon as he was outside, however, he stopped, directionless. Where would Angel have gone? He ran his hands through his hair, looking anxiously in both directions down the street, and let out a frustrated growl as his mind remained unhelpfully blank.

Well, if nothing else, he had a good guess where his father would be. And if Nathan could find his father, he could make sure his father stayed away from Angel. With that thought to direct his steps, Nathan set out for the saloon.

When he arrived at the saloon, it was nearly empty. The only person there was the bartender.

"Has my father been in here?" Nathan asked, not bothering to clarify who his father was—he knew James was well-acquainted with the bartender. James had spent many hours in this saloon over the years.

The bartender nodded. "The sheriff and his deputy came by and picked him up this morning. You can find him at the jail if you want —they are holding him there until the trial."

Nathan breathed a sigh of relief. If his father was already at the jail, he wouldn't be able to harm Angel.

"The trial," Nathan asked, "when is it to be?"

The bartender looked at him with a guarded expression, as though unsure how Nathan would react. "Well, it's almost noon now, so here in about an hour."

"That's sooner than I expected," Nathan said slowly.

The bartender shrugged. "I think they wanted to get it over with as soon as they could, knowing James and all." He shot a glance at Nathan. "I'm sorry if I am giving you bad news."

Shaking his head, Nathan answered, glancing back at the bartender as he walked toward the exit. "There's nothing to apologize for. You told me what I came here to find out, and I thank you for that."

∼

ANGEL HAD GONE to the cabin, hoping to see Nathan for two reasons. The first was James's trial. Nathan had a right to know that his father was being brought in and that his father's trial had already been scheduled for that same day. The second reason—the reason she kept pushed to the back of her mind—was that Angel wanted to tell Nathan the truth about his father and her baby before he heard it from someone else.

She knew almost as soon as she arrived at the farm that Nathan was not there. The cabin's windows were dark, and the mare was missing from the barn. Angel glanced anxiously up at the sun, noting its position in the sky. The trial would be starting soon. She would barely have enough time to make it to the courthouse if she left now, but there would be no time to look for Nathan once she arrived in town.

There was no doubt in Angel's mind that Nathan was already in town, or at least on his way to town, although she wasn't sure how they could have missed each other on the road. The thought calmed Angel temporarily—she knew that if Nathan was in town, someone would have told him about the trial.

And then with a chill that started from the inside and worked its way out, she was forced to remember her role in the trial. Angel had been able to push the thought aside, directing her energy toward finding Nathan to tell him about his father's trial. Now, she was left with nothing to distract her from her secondary concern—telling Nathan the truth about his father and her baby before he learned it from someone else.

I should have told Nathan as soon as I realized it was his father.

Those were the words that ran, over and over again, through Angel's mind as she rode back to town. She didn't want to push the horse, or herself—her body had only just begun to feel like it was fully recovering from the baby's delivery—so she settled for a fast walk, growing more and more agitated as they drew nearer and nearer to town, as the appointed time for the trial edged closer and closer, and as she grew less and less sure she would make it to the courthouse in time, let alone with time to speak with Nathan beforehand.

When she finally arrived at the courthouse, Angel was relieved to see that there were still a few stragglers entering the building. She slid off the horse and looped the reins around a hitching post, then fairly ran up the stairs and into courtroom. As she entered, the judge looked disapprovingly at her flushed cheeks, and Angel found herself self-consciously smoothing her hair and the front of her dress as she looked around for Clark and Olivia and Nathan.

They were sitting near the front of the courtroom. Olivia noticed Angel first and waved her over with a look of relief. Angel sat beside Olivia, looking across her to where Nathan sat.

"Where have you been? We were worried," Olivia hissed underneath the murmuring buzz of the room.

At Olivia's tone, Angel's eyes hardened, and she struggled to keep the edge from her voice as she answered, "Worried about me? Or worried that I was planning to back out of my decision to testify against James?"

Olivia's expression softened, although the softness had a forced look about it, and the edge in her voice matched Angel's own. "We were worried for you, Nathan especially. When he arrived at the house this morning and you weren't there, he was terrified you would come across James and come to harm. He fairly ran from the house to look for you."

Still, Angel held Olivia's gaze. Finally, Olivia tore her gaze away first. "I will not deny the thought had crossed my mind that you might have changed your mind about testifying," she admitted, "but our first concern was for you."

Angel shook her head, then glanced to the side of the room where James sat. Calm. Relaxed. Confident. He caught her eye and winked. Angel jerked her gaze away from him and stared straight ahead at the front of the room, her heart pounding in her chest.

"I apologize," Angel said to Olivia, and Olivia relaxed. "I am . . ." Her voice trailed off and she tried to form the words to describe exactly what she was. Afraid? Uncertain? Scarcely able to breathe?

Understanding softened Olivia's face, and then she said with urgency, "You must speak with Nathan before the trial begins."

Immediately, Oliva turned to Nathan, motioning for him to switch places with her. A wave of fear washed over Angel as Nathan moved to stand and Olivia slid by him on the bench. Angel's mouth was dry. She felt dizzy and her breaths did not seem to come quickly enough. When Nathan sat, he glanced at her, smiling, his expression of relief mirroring the look Olivia had given Angel. Then, as he saw Angel's condition he asked in concern, "Are you all right?"

Angel shook her head, forcing herself to breathe slowly, counting the length of each breath. The trial had come together rapidly—more rapidly than Angel had even thought possible. When she had agreed to testify against James, she had thought she would have time to speak with Nathan, to gather her thoughts, but James, who the sheriff had apparently found drinking indifferently in the saloon, had been brought in that very morning without struggle only minutes after Clark had spoken with the sheriff. Angel marveled at James's easy demeanor, wondering uneasily whether it was a perfectly crafted act or if he was truly as unconcerned as he appeared.

Now, when the scarcest moment of opportunity for Angel to tell Nathan the truth finally presented itself, she was unable to do so—even knowing with complete and total certainty that if she didn't tell Nathan now, he would hear the truth in just a few minutes.

In those few minutes, Angel tried over and over to tell Nathan the truth, knowing that the misery she felt at that moment could never compare to the misery she would feel if the trial began before she spoke to Nathan, but fear petrified her, justifying her silence, reasoning that it would be better to wait, and before she could force herself to speak, the opportunity had passed. The judge stood to address the room, and almost immediately the room fell silent.

She had been right. This was worse. Far, far worse. Panic seized her, and she turned to Nathan. "There's something I need to tell you." She wanted to run, but she was surrounded by people pressing in on her.

Angel's head felt light, distant, and her voice sounded strange and breathy, even to herself, and Nathan looked at her with increasing concern.

"What in the name of—" he said anxiously.

"We call Angel Bernard to the stand," a voice from the front of the room interrupted, and time seemed to slow as Angel stood unsteadily. Shock spread across Nathan's face.

"I'm sorry," Angel whispered, so quietly that the words were more mouthed than spoken, and then walked to the front of the room.

18

The part of me that knows I could have just dropped her off at home without anything else happening, the part of me that knows I could have stopped myself from pulling the trigger on that bartender, the part of me that knows I could have let my son leave with my brother after Effie died . . . that part of me refuses to drown.

"MISS BERNARD, were you a witness to the murder of Thomas Bernard?"

"Yes," Angel whispered. Nathan stared at her as though he had never before seen her in his life.

"Louder, please, Miss."

"Yes," she repeated, her voice sounding strained to her own ears.

"What was your relationship to Mr. Bernard?"

"He is—was—my uncle, sir."

"How did you come to be at the scene of the crime, Miss Bernard?"

Angel flushed. "I lived at the saloon with my uncle after my parents died. The day my uncle was killed, I heard yelling in the main room downstairs, so I went to see what was happening."

She chanced a glance at Nathan. He was still looking at her like he might a stranger, and Angel felt her blush deepen.

"Why didn't you come forward with this information before now?" the man questioning her continued.

Angel started. She had not expected that particular question, although she supposed she should have. "Sir," she began slowly, "I . . . didn't realize who the person was who had killed my uncle. When I came down to check on my uncle, I was injured. I fell and hit my head. Even now, some of my memories are fuzzy. But I do remember now the man who killed my uncle."

"And what exactly prompted this memory of your uncle's murderer?" Disdain dripped from the man's voice. It was clear he placed little faith in the truthfulness of Angel's testimony.

"I saw him. He spoke to me, and I recognized him."

"And is the man who shot Thomas Bernard in this room?"

"Yes."

"Will you please point him out?"

Angel pointed to Nathan's father, and said, "That man there, sir. James Evans."

"What words would you offer to defend yourself?" The man spoke brusquely to Nathan's father.

James smiled and stood, and Angel felt the pit of her stomach drop. "Your Honor, I would offer truth. This woman is an unreliable witness. I regret to call the character of a woman into question, sir, but would an honorable woman, niece or not, live in a saloon?" James paused, then continued. "Normally I would hesitate to disclose this information for the sake of discretion—perhaps the members of the fairer sex should be allowed to leave the room before we continue?"

The judge's eyes narrowed, but he waved James on.

"No?" James asked, then sighed as though he were speaking only with great reluctance and regret. "Well then, if you are certain, I suppose I must continue. This woman—Angel—and I were lovers.

We did not part ways on pleasant terms. I suppose that is why she persists in telling these stories about me. I do not doubt she believes the things she says—I can only imagine the trauma that would have arisen from witnessing the murder of her uncle and how it would have affected her delicate female memory. I make no claims to be a good man, Your Honor, but this woman imagines I have committed more wrongs than I truly have."

Angel's mouth fell open, and she felt a sharp intake of breath. The white noise of the room suddenly rose, becoming a near physical force. But she didn't care. The only reaction she cared about was Nathan's. She looked over Clark and Olivia, sitting between herself and Nathan, to finally meet Nathan's eyes, dark with shock, eyebrows close together.

The judge banged his gavel down, quieting the buzzing crowd. "Silence," he bellowed. He looked coldly at Angel. "Is what he says true, Miss? Did you have"—his voice quieted as he uncomfortably whispered the word, "relations"—then rose again as he continued—"with this man?"

Angel was stunned. She barely managed to speak as she tried to explain. "That isn't what happened."

The judge glowered at her. "This is a simple question, Miss. I suggest you answer it. Did you or did you not have relations with this man—yes or no?"

Angel stared at him, mouth still open. The room was silent as she whispered, "Yes, but—"

The room roared, and her voice was swallowed in the noise as she screamed, "But it wasn't my choice."

No one heard her.

Again the judge banged his gavel down until reasonable quiet had resumed. "We will take a short recess. You"—he motioned to James—"will remain here with me. You"—he motioned to Angel, his voice growing colder and speaking with distaste—"may take your leave."

Above the crowd, James met Angel's eyes. And smiled.

NATHAN CURTLY KNOCKED TWICE on the door of room before pushing it open. Angel had fled the courtroom as soon as she had been dismissed by the judge, but Nathan had easily guessed where he would find her. He had spoken briefly to Clark and Olivia, who had nodded their assent during the chaos that had followed Angel's admission, and then Nathan had come straight to their house to speak with Angel. Clark and Olivia had remained to anxiously await the result of the trial.

Angel's eyes were wild as she turned toward the sound of the opening door. As she saw that it was Nathan, she relaxed briefly, then tensed and turned back to her work. Nathan glanced around. Even though Angel had few belongings, the room looked as though it had been struck by a small whirlwind. She clearly intended to ready herself to leave as soon as possible. Nathan wondered if she had intended to say goodbye.

Leaving the door open, he silently walked into the room and sat down on a chair next to the desk, watching her. She ignored him for some time, but when he remained, Angel gave a sigh of resignation and turned to face him. As she turned, Nathan noticed a piece of paper resting on the desk out of the corner of his eye. The ink on the page had not even dried yet. Angel stiffened as she realized the letter had caught his attention, and without asking, Nathan began to read.

My—but the "My" had been hastily scratched out, and the letter began—*Dearest Nathan, I promised you that I would not leave without saying goodbye. I hope you will someday forgive me for saying in writing what I cannot bring myself to say out loud . . .*

He didn't read any further but set the letter down back in its place.

"You know, I can't figure out whether you are running from my father, or me," Nathan said quietly, the injury of the letter plain in his voice.

Angel stiffened, and she planted her feet squarely, as though bracing herself to stand against whatever words he might speak. Her eyes pleaded with him not to ask the question that must have been plain in his eyes. But he needed to know.

"How long have you known it was my father?" he asked quietly. Angel shook her head, looking away, but it was more a denial of the question than an answer, and Nathan knew it. His temper flashed, and almost simultaneously he rose from his seat at the desk and slammed the palm of hand down onto it. The wooden feet of the desk squeaked in protest as they skidded against the floor.

"How long?" Nathan asked again, and this time there was nothing quiet about his voice. Still, Angel stared at the floor. She didn't respond.

"Angel."

Nathan's voice around her name held a pull she could no longer ignore, and slowly she raised her eyes to meet his. Her eyes were wide-open, and she looked up at the ceiling, trying to contain the water they held. Then she blinked, and a tear slid out of the corner of her eye and down her cheek. She did not wipe it away.

"Don't play games with me, Angel. I deserve the truth."

At his words, Angel raised her chin, setting her jaw.

Nathan impatiently repeated the question one last time, speaking with almost deafening silence, "How long have you known?"

Angel matched his gaze, then spat, "Do you truly believe this is all a game to me—that I've found some twisted delight in your father's depravity? You are still the boy who found me on the side of the road, who played with cruel words and made accusations he knew nothing of. You should know better, Nathan. I've never played games with you."

The words stung Nathan, but he repeated stubbornly, "Then answer the question. How long?"

Angel took a step forward. She searched his face for what seemed like forever, then finally answered, "Since your father came back into town."

Nathan didn't know what he had expected, but he hadn't expected that answer. He stared at Angel, understanding dawning on him. He couldn't keep the bitterness from his voice as he continued speaking. "The whole time, my father stood there laughing, asking you if I knew. I had no idea what he was talking about, and you never told me. I must have looked the fool."

He turned, coat in hand, poised to walk out the door. He clenched his jaw, biting his tongue against the words he wanted to say. He looked back at Angel, and when his eyes met hers, she seemed to crumple, but Nathan was unmoved. He hated his father, he hated that Angel hadn't told him what his father had done, and more than anything, he despised himself for missing the truth that had stared him in the face. And he didn't care if Angel knew it.

"What he said wasn't true," she whispered. "It wasn't by choice."

Nathan didn't look at her. "I know," he said, "but you should have told me it was him."

And then he walked out the door.

NATHAN FELT the echo of the wooden floor against the heels of his shoes as he stepped into the saloon, doors swinging behind him. It was nearly empty, and he drew the attention of the bartender as he sank down to sit on the barstool. The bartender did a double take as he recognized Nathan, then relaxed. He walked up to stand in front of Nathan, polishing a glass with an old rag as he did so.

"Thought you were your father there for a minute," the bartender said conversationally.

When Nathan turned sullen eyes toward him, the bartender added with a smile, "I'm sure glad you're not."

When Nathan didn't reply, the bartender asked, "What can I do for you, son?"

Nathan held the bartender's eyes for a moment, then said, "I need a whiskey."

The bartender leaned back almost imperceptibly at Nathan's words. He turned to grab a bottle and then, with a smooth and practiced motion, wiped off a glass and placed it in front of Nathan.

"Whiskey, eh? That always was your father's drink of choice," the bartender said casually as he poured the shot.

Nathan considered the amber liquid as he twirled the glass between his fingers. "Really?" His tone was distracted, but it held the bite of sarcasm. "I didn't know that."

The bartender eyed Nathan, looking as though he was going to speak again, but before he could, he was called away by another customer. Nathan tilted the glass up until just the corner was resting against the wood of the bar. The edges of the glass shone, catching even the dim light of the saloon. As he stared at the glass, his reflection—his father—stared back at him. With an exhale of frustration, Nathan set the shot glass down harder than he needed to. When the bartender returned, Nathan was still staring into the glass, spinning it back and forth on the bar. The bartender watched for a while, then finally asked, "You sure you want to be here, son?"

"Yeah," Nathan answered without looking at him.

"You sure you want to drink that?"

Finally, Nathan looked up from the drink and met the bartender's eyes. "I never said anything about drinking."

Nathan lifted the shot glass away from the bar and tilted it so that the whiskey trickled out, catching the light and sending it dancing as the droplets fell to the floor. Then he set it back on the bar in front of him.

Gesturing to the now-empty glass, he said, "Pour another one."

The bartender's eyes narrowed, but he did as Nathan had asked. Again, Nathan poured the glass out, and again, he motioned for it to be refilled.

"This is a waste of good whiskey," the bartender protested. "And you're making the floor a right mess."

"I'm paying you for the whiskey, aren't I?" Nathan asked. The bartender nodded. "And you can't tell me this floor hasn't seen worse."

The bartender hesitated but couldn't deny what Nathan had said.

Nathan motioned from the bottle of whiskey to the glass. "Pour it."

Slowly, the bartender complied. He watched without words as Nathan emptied the shot glass for the third time. Nathan opened his mouth to speak, but before he could make his request, the bartender held up his hands. "I know, I know, pour it."

After he had filled the glass, he eyed Nathan, then spoke, sarcasm lacing his voice. "Shall I leave the bottle?"

Nathan nodded, and the bartender, shaking his head, set the whiskey in front of Nathan and walked away.

With every shot Nathan poured out, memories flooded his mind. His father, passed out on the floor of the cabin. The ache of his bruised muscles from every beating his father had given him. The whispers that had followed him around town after his mother's death like a swarm of buzzing insects. The sweat and blood he had poured into the homestead that was still in his father's name. The fear in Angel's eyes when she had looked at him for the first time after seeing his father.

Some minutes later, the bartender returned to a still-sober Nathan, a nearly empty bottle of whiskey, and a spreading dark stain on the floor.

"What do I owe you for the glass?" Nathan asked.

"The glass?" the bartender repeated, confusion covering his face. Nathan dropped the glass on the floor, and the crunch of breaking glass filled the silent air as he ground the heel of his boot against it and into the floor. Never again.

The bartender was silent for a long moment, then said, "I'll put it on your tab."

"Much obliged." Nathan nodded as he stood to leave.

"Nathan." The bartender's voice caused Nathan to pause in his exit, and he turned his head slightly toward the sound.

"You spend too much time trying to prove what anyone with a brain can already see—you're not James. You aren't him, and you aren't like him. Go home and get some rest. Sleep off whatever's ailing you. You won't find any answers in the whiskey, and there's already a big enough mess on the floor."

NATHAN'S WORDS plagued Angel even as she continued readying herself to leave. Who was she running from—Nathan or his father? James terrified her. There was no question about that. Her stomach clenched whenever she thought of the man. But as afraid as she was of James, Angel had been even more afraid of what Nathan's reaction would be to learning the truth about his father.

But Nathan hadn't reacted with the disgust she had feared. In fact, he hadn't treated her much differently at all. He had been angry that Angel hadn't told him the entire truth sooner and hurt that she had planned to leave without saying goodbye, but he had barely, if at all, reacted to the revelation of the identity of the father of Angel's baby.

The word Nathan had used—running—echoed over and over in her mind. She had run from the saloon. She had run from the people in her old town, from what they thought of her and would have thought when they learned she was pregnant. She had run from James. She had run from Nathan. She was so tired of running.

With one swift motion, she picked up the letter she had written to Nathan and crumpled it. Suddenly, even though she still cared what Nathan might think when all was said and done, she didn't care in the same way. If he thought so little of her, she would make him say it to her face, rather than sparing him the trouble by leaving before he could say it. If he was going to break her heart, she would at least make it uncomfortable for him. And if he didn't, well, then . . . that would certainly be a more pleasant outcome, and she would cross that bridge when she came to it.

Angel rushed out of her room and down the stairs, holding the banister with one hand and the hem of her dress up with the other.

"Where are you going?" Olivia asked.

Without slowing, Angel answered, "To see the judge."

"What for?"

On her way out the door, Angel paused for just a moment. "I am tired of running away."

And then the door closed and Angel was running to the courthouse. For the first time, she didn't care what anyone would say about her loose braid, or the unladylike way she was dashing down the street, or what had happened between herself and James. For the first time, even though her breaths were heavy, and she didn't know what would happen after this day, she felt free.

19

I *know I am not a good man. I know some people might say I could change. I also know I never will.*

"Sɪʀ?" Angel asked, standing in the doorway to where the judge sat. He looked up from his writing but, when he saw who it was, looked back down at the paper in front of him and began methodically scratching out words again.

"You should not be here," he grunted, dismissing her.

She took a step into the room, and he again looked up. "I could have you removed from this property," he warned.

"Sir," Angel said again, pleading, "please listen to what I have to say. No matter what he said, James Evans and I were never lovers."

The judge's expression grew dangerous. "You spoke under oath, Miss. If you lied—"

"Your Honor, with all due respect, I did not lie," Angel said firmly, "but what you heard today was not the truth."

The judge looked sharply up at her. And then, for the first time, the judge set down his pen and turned his full attention on Angel. Leaning back in his chair, he said, "I am listening. Go on."

"James and I were not lovers. I came downstairs to see what was happening, and when James saw me, he shot my uncle in front of me, and then he attacked and forced me."

The judge's face grew taught. "What reason do I have to believe this?" he asked.

Angel paused, then spoke. "You do not know the kind of person I am, but you do know the kind of man James is. Is it so difficult for you to believe the things I am saying are true?"

CLARK FOUND Nathan sitting on the ground outside the fence in front of his and Olivia's house. He didn't ask why Nathan was not inside.

"You're in town late," he observed, sitting down beside him.

Nathan gave him a sideways glance. "Can't go home." His voice was low and strained.

"James," Clark stated without question, and Nathan nodded. "Scared?"

Nathan shot Clark an irritated look and shook his head like a horse trying to lose a persistent fly. "Not scared. Just not a fool."

One corner of Clark's mouth lifted slightly, then he asked, "Did you speak with Angel?"

Again, Nathan nodded dully.

"I take it your conversation did not go well?"

Nathan couldn't bring himself to answer, and he continued staring down at the ground in front of him.

Clark nodded, taking Nathan's silence as confirmation. The two sat in silence, Clark seeming to fight some inner battle. Finally, he said, "I never wanted you to know what I'm about to tell you, Nathan. When Olivia and I first came back, I told you there were some things even you didn't know about your father. I thought it was for the best to keep them from you. But now . . ." Clark took a deep breath, then said, "Felicity is not my daughter—not in the traditional sense, anyway."

Nathan jerked around to stare at Clark. "How is that possible? I mean, if not you, then who . . ."

His voice trailed off as an awful suspicion started to form in the back of his mind. Clark must have seen the look of dawning horror because he nodded, then said, "Felicity is James's daughter, Nathan. She is your half sister."

Stunned, Nathan asked, "My father and Olivia?"

"Olivia, much like Angel, was not given any choice," Clark said quietly.

Nathan ran his hands through his hair. "Every time . . ." he said bitterly. "Every. Single. Time I think my father can't get any worse, he does."

Clark interrupted his thoughts, his eyes intent. "I need you to understand, Nathan—I do not tell you this to grow your hatred of your father. I tell you because I believe I understand a small part of what you are feeling. We have not seen eye to eye on many things, but if you only ever believe one thing I tell you, believe this: if you care for Angel at all, in any way—if you want any sort of future with her—you must learn to separate your father's influence from her— much the way she has done for you, I would suspect, in many ways."

Clark stood, turning to go inside, then paused. "And I would guess you do not have much time to learn how to do that."

As Clark spoke, Nathan had been struck by another memory— the memory of a young girl sitting with him on the front steps of a saloon. Angel.

He had to find her. Nathan stood frantically, then realized that she was most likely inside the building right in front of him. Clark had turned to watch him when he had heard Nathan stand, and Nathan met his eyes.

"Can I please come in?" Nathan asked.

"Of course." Clark smiled his approval, and the warmth of his expression gave Nathan a sudden burst of courage.

ANGEL WAS NOT at Clark and Olivia's when Nathan entered their home. After Olivia assured Nathan that Angel had not mysteriously disappeared—although she declined to tell Nathan exactly where Angel had gone—Nathan sat down at the table to wait. Olivia kept herself busy, bustling around the kitchen, and when she spoke her voice was light, but Nathan could see the concern written across both her face and Clark's.

When Angel walked through the door, she halted midstride—stunned by Nathan's presence. And then, almost all at once, gladness, and then apprehension, and then a flat lack of expression passed over her face. Olivia cheerfully announced dinner, and the four of them uncomfortably sat down together.

"How did your visit go, dear?" Olivia asked Angel.

"Visit?" Nathan asked before Angel could answer.

"I went to see the judge." Angel's words were clipped.

Nathan stared at her. "You went to see the judge?" he repeated incredulously.

Angel eyed him coolly. "Yes."

"Why?" Nathan asked.

"I thought he should know the truth before he let James go. I am tired of running, and I am done being afraid." She spoke to the table, but her words were sharp, pointed—clearly directed at Nathan. At once he felt a surge of hope.

"What did he say?" Nathan pressed, but before Angel could answer, the door swung slowly open, and Nathan and Angel both turned toward the sound. With the familiarity of someone who had walked through the door many times before, a man strode through the door, the heels of his boots clipping the wooden floor. As one, the four of them rose from the table.

James.

"A family dinner? And I wasn't even invited." James clucked his tongue. "Don't worry, I won't be here long. I hear the sheriff is looking for me again and that I have you to thank for that." Here, he nodded at Angel, then continued. "Besides, I've just come to claim what's mine."

Nathan glanced at Angel, then Olivia. Their paleness mirrored one another's. Clark's color, on the other hand, had darkened significantly.

James turned in a circle, surveying his surroundings, then stopped. His gaze settled on each of them in turn, and then he chuckled softly, almost to himself.

"What, pray tell," Clark asked tersely, "do you find so amusing, James?"

James started, feigning surprise as though he had been so involved in his own musings that he had forgotten their presence. "Oh, nothing." He smiled. "I was just recalling a silly rhyme. How does it go, now?" he asked himself. "Something old." He nodded at Nathan. "And something new." He nodded toward Angel. "Something borrowed." He tipped his hat toward Olivia and she flushed. "And Clark, you've even got the something blue."

Clark glanced down at the blue fabric of his shirt with chagrin, and James barked his laughter, clapping a hand on his knee as though the mirth of the situation was too much for him to contain.

Then, James's demeanor abruptly changed.

"What are you doing here?" he snarled at Clark and Olivia. "Didn't I tell you if you ever came back, I'd kill you?"

Clark stepped between James and Olivia. "We could ask the same of you, James. Why are you here?"

James considered Clark for a long moment, eyes narrowed. When he spoke, he drawled the words slowly, mockingly. "I already told you. I'm here to claim what's mine."

"And what might that be?" Clark asked.

Nathan glanced at Angel. She breathed shallowly as they all waited for James's reply. He carefully considered each of them in turn, and some of his initial joviality returned.

"Well, now, that's a funny question—" he began, smiling, but Clark cut him off.

"James," he spoke in a warning tone, and James whirled around to face him, stepping closer and closer until he was within arm's reach of Clark. Still, Clark stood motionless. Nathan wondered at his control.

James spat on the floor. Clark's eyes never left James's, but Nathan glanced down to see the spittle land on the floor next to Clark's foot. James shoved Clark backward. Clark absorbed the shock, taking one step back, and only one step, before he stood again, resolutely meeting James's gaze.

"I'm here to collect my son and the deed to my land. You have any objection to that?" James finally asked.

Clark snorted. "Whether or not I do, I suspect Nathan might, and he is more than old enough to make his own decision in that regard."

"He'll come with me," James said.

"And if I don't?" Nathan asked quietly. "That land is mine by law, and I have no intention of handing it over to you."

James looked at him almost pityingly as he slid a gun out from under the coat he was wearing. The gun drew their eyes like a magnet, and James set it on the table in front of him. The weapon's weight connected with the table's surface with a metallic thud.

"You will," James said softly.

At that moment, Nathan realized something. James had been almost constantly moving since he had arrived. They all—with the exception of Clark—had stood nearly frozen in place, hypnotized. And now Angel was too near.

Nathan's awareness and sudden tension drew James's attention. As he followed Nathan's gaze, his own attention landed on Angel. Before she could move, he slid an arm around her waist, his fingers moving across her back, curving into her side and pulling her close to him. Nathan stiffened. James looked down at Angel and smiled.

"Hello again, Angel-no-more," his father breathed.

Nathan moved to pick up the gun, but Olivia was faster. She picked up the gun and leveled it at James with a steady hand. Mild surprise showed on James's face, and he raised his free hand, palm out, disarmingly.

"Let her go, James," Olivia said calmly.

Nathan wondered what Olivia was thinking. Why should his father listen to her? Olivia wasn't the type to pull the trigger.

And yet, his father's hold on Angel loosened almost imperceptibly for just a moment before tightening again. Nathan stared at Olivia as she continued speaking conversationally to his father.

"You know I won't miss. Someone I once cared about taught me well. Do you remember that day, James? I do, quite well. I think I was even a better shot than you, and that is saying something."

For the first time, Nathan noticed how Olivia held the gun. Confidently. Casually. Without fear.

James looked at Olivia with a funny expression. "Of everything I've done," he said quietly, "hurting you is the one thing I regret the most."

Whatever Olivia had been expecting, that was not it. A myriad of expressions flew over her face before settling on fury.

"What is wrong with you, James?" she spat. "Is that some sort of apology that is supposed to make it all right?"

"No." James shook his head. "I'm not apologizing. I know it wouldn't make a difference. I just thought you should know the truth." Then he laughed, releasing Angel and pushing her away. "Go ahead, Livvy, shoot me."

Olivia's eyes narrowed. "If you're in such a truth-telling mood, tell me what happened to my sister."

Again, James gave Olivia a funny look, hedging his response with snideness. "She died, Livvy. Shouldn't you know that? Being—what would you call it—your sister's keeper and all?"

Olivia hissed out her breath, tightening her grip on the gun. Nathan began to rethink his earlier assessment, wondering if Olivia would pull the trigger after all.

"I'll ask you one more time, James. Did you kill Effie?" Olivia asked.

James looked at her for a long moment, then answered, "No."

Nathan's head jerked up in shock. "You didn't?"

"No," James said, and this time his voice held the sarcasm Nathan had expected. "I believe I just said that."

"Then what happened?" Nathan asked.

Again, James paused. "She jumped."

The room was silent as they soaked in James's words. Finally, Olivia croaked out a reply, "I don't believe you."

James shrugged. "Suit yourself. Believe me or don't, but what I just told you is the only truth you'll ever know."

Olivia's face was cold. "I could make you tell me."

"Even if I thought you had it in you to try, the only thing you would succeed in making me tell you would be what you want to hear," James challenged her, "and I don't know what that is, Livvy. Unless," he said suggestively, "you want to hear me call you darlin' again."

"Enough!" Clark's booming voice cut through James's slithered words. James fell silent, but looked unconcerned. Nathan stared at him. Even with the four of them to his one and a gun pointed directly at him, James seemed to be completely in control. Nathan eyed the gun Olivia held, wondering if it was even loaded and whether his father had another concealed somewhere on his person.

"Are you going to kill me, little brother?" James asked. "Have you already forgotten how I saved your life all those years ago?"

"You've worn out that excuse many times over, James. And it's been years since you've been my brother," Clark snarled.

James's eyes narrowed, and a slow smile spread across his face as he asked, "And tell me, little brother, when exactly did that change? I'd gamble you can name the day."

Clark hesitated, then answered slowly, "The day you saved my life."

James turned away from Clark to speak to the others in the room. His voice was almost friendly. "Has my little brother shared this story with you? It's a good one."

Clark flushed, and when no one spoke, James's voice hardened, and he spoke with an edge. "Well then, let me enlighten you all. When I was about fourteen—what would that have made you, little brother, thirteen?—we had a spring where the river and all the creeks were higher than they'd ever been. We'd had more snow than usual that winter, and then spring came fast. There was a Chinook wind that blew all day and night, and the snow all melted at once. Even inside the cabin, you could hear the roar of water all through the night. The next day, I happened across Clark, and what was he doing but showing off for little Livvy here—walking across a tree trunk that had fallen across the water—fool thing to do. It was quite the sight—Livvy begging him to come back to safety, Clark grinning back at her . . . and then slipping on a wet spot and falling into the water. I jumped in after him. The water was so fast it was close to a quarter mile before we made it to the bank, both of us nearly drowned.

"When we finally made it back to the cabin, our father was there. He took one look at Clark, yelled at him to put some dry clothes on, and then took after me with his belt because I hadn't kept my younger brother—the best son he had—from getting himself into such a fool situation.

"And Clark stood there and watched."

James smiled at their stunned silence, then his voice hardened as he said, "No, little brother, every single day that you are alive, that excuse will never be worn out."

James's words had clearly rubbed a raw spot in Clark's memory—his expression was one of pure anguish. "You changed that day," Clark said quietly. "I could see it in your eyes—you weren't my brother anymore." Then he seemed to plead with James. "I didn't know how to stop our father."

James spat on the floor, and his words were venomous. "No, you were afraid to."

Clark didn't argue with James's accusation, and the absence of Clark's denial hung heavy in the air. "I'm sorry," he whispered.

The only acknowledgement James gave Clark's words was a bare flicker of his eyes in Clark's direction. But then, James's expression abruptly changed again, and he continued speaking as though he hadn't heard Clark at all. Though he spoke to the room, his words were plainly meant for Olivia.

"I really did care for Effie, you know." He laughed at Olivia's look of disbelief. "Oh, I know what you think, Livvy. I hated you. You and

Clark both. But you, Livvy," he said, turning back to Olivia, "after I saw how scared you looked that day you got married—I know you didn't know I was there—I realized you hadn't been fooling around behind my back with my good-for-nothing brother. No woman who'd had any . . . experience . . . with the man they were marrying would look so terrified on their wedding day. I was good and sober that day, and I realized I'd made a mistake."

He didn't seem to notice the reactions his words had evoked from Olivia and Clark as he continued. "Then there was Effie. Your sister," James scoffed, almost to himself. "I tried to stay away from her at first, wanted nothing to do with her, but she was always around, always wanting to know more about me, and you, and Clark. Teasing and flirting when I'd get angry with her for asking so many questions." James grimaced. "After we were married, I did catch her with another man—that sorry excuse for a bartender. You seemed well acquainted with him, Angel-no-more."

James nodded at her, and Angel felt a chill shoot through her body. That was the reason James had shot Tom?

Olivia's face was pale with shock. "Effie . . . wouldn't have done that."

James tsked at her. "And yet she did."

"You admit you did kill her then?" Olivia accused.

"No," James said impatiently, "I already told you I didn't kill Effie. She jumped off that cliff all on her own."

Then he shrugged his shoulders. "I am what I am, Livvy. You should know that. You all think you're so different from me. Well, you're not. Someday you'll see."

Something snapped inside Nathan. He had listened to enough, seen enough, and now understood enough. He held out his hand to Olivia. "Give me the gun."

Olivia hesitated, opening her mouth to protest. Something in Nathan's eyes stopped her, and she mutely handed him the weapon. He turned his eyes toward his father, and then, without looking away, raised the gun toward the ceiling and pulled the trigger six times.

No shot came. Only the snap of hammer on metal.

James had briefly smiled as Nathan had begun to raise the pistol, but his smile had turned to a frown when the gun's trajectory had moved beyond him to the ceiling. Now, he scowled. It was, Nathan realized, the first time since James had first walked into the room that he had seemed anything less than completely in control. Nathan smiled in grim satisfaction.

James hissed through his teeth, then smiled, speaking to Nathan, but gesturing toward the others and resuming his conversational tone. "What of them, Nathan? What will you do when the gun is loaded and it's in my hand? Would you kill me—your own father—to protect them?" James asked curiously.

Nathan spoke evenly, deliberately, emphasizing each word. "They are more my family now than you ever have been, James."

James's eyes narrowed as Nathan called him by his name, but he persisted. "You didn't answer the question. Would you kill me to protect these people?"

Nathan hesitated for only a moment, but it was a moment too long, and James said contemptuously, "That's what I thought."

"What did you think?" Nathan asked irritably.

James paused, then drawled, "I've overstayed my welcome. I believe I will be on my way for now."

Clark made a choking noise as James moved to leave. James paused, turning slightly, then asked innocently, "I am free to go, am I not, brother? After all"—he shrugged, motioning toward the empty gun Nathan still held—"you are a man of principle. I am unarmed, and you wouldn't harm an unarmed man."

ANGEL WATCHED James's back as he left. It was the same silhouette that had haunted her since that day seven months ago. The same silhouette that had left her lying motionless on the floor, broken like the glass strewn around her.

"No," she whispered. She couldn't help following as James walked out the door. Then she spoke again, louder this time. "No."

The sound wasn't loud, barely raised above conversational tones, but it made James pause. He turned to look at Angel, and she felt sharp shards of ice lance through her veins.

"No, what?" he asked, his tone dangerous.

"No, you don't win," Angel said. Her mouth and throat were dry, and the words croaked past her lips. But they were louder than a whisper.

James stared at her, then laughed. "And what exactly don't I win, Angel-no-more?" He began walking back toward her. Her heart thudded against her chest, feeling off rhythm and horribly loud. "Olivia and Clark—their marriage is a farce. Clark always has been and always will have been Olivia's second choice. I know it, Olivia knows it, and Clark knows it."

James pulled a gun from underneath his coat pocket as he walked —so he had been armed. He continued. "Nathan—he is just like me. He just hasn't figured it out yet. And you, Angel-no-more, you are the best of the lot. Pregnant with one of my sons and in love with the other."

He was close enough to touch. James took one more step, then took Angel's hand, wrapping her fingers around the stock of the gun and placing the open end of the barrel against his chest.

"How are you going to keep me from winning, Angel-no-more? Are you going to kill me?" James whispered.

"Angel," the voice came softly. Nathan. She hadn't noticed he had come up behind her. Something told her Clark and Olivia were standing behind her as well, silent and breathless.

"Don't shoot him, Angel." The voice was pleading, and it stung, pricking her eyes and making them water.

James held Angel's eyes.

"Go ahead," James challenged her. "Shoot me."

Angel stared at Nathan's father. She had thought she knew exactly who he was—what he was. She had been wrong. There was no fiendish light in his eyes, only darkness and death. His were the eyes and misery of a corroded and decaying soul, of one who despised life yet fought for it. She wasn't sure which was worse—the vision she had held of a man who took pleasure in cruelty, or this new image of a man who was cruel because it was easier to justify, and entice others to do the same, than to do any differently.

"No," she whispered, then spoke again, louder this time as she realized she wasn't afraid. "No." James's eyes darkened. "You are wrong. Nathan is nothing like you. Olivia loves Clark more than she ever loved you. And I am not broken. This isn't Nathan's tragedy, or Clark's tragedy, or Olivia's tragedy. James, it's not even my tragedy— it's yours."

A strange look flitted over James's face, then vanished. He snorted, pulling the gun from Angel's grasp and turning it around to face her. "You sure do have a smart mouth on you, Angel-no-more."

Angel met his gaze evenly, refusing to flinch. And as James stared at her, the strange look came over his face again. He shook his head. The movement was so slight Angel hardly saw it, even though they stood face-to-face. Even though he was looking straight at her, his eyes were distant. Then, almost to himself, James said, "I can hardly remember . . ."

As he spoke, his eyes searched her face, and he raised a hand and placed the gun back in Angel's grasp, then reached toward her as though he were going to lay his hand against her cheek. This time, Angel did step back.

With Angel's movement, James suddenly focused on her. "Why did I shoot him?" he asked.

A slow anger started to burn inside Angel's chest, and her hands clenched into fists at her sides, but her voice was steady as she replied, "Effie?"

James nodded. "Probably."

Then James seemed to shake himself from his trance and looked at each of them in turn. "I'll be on my way now. I'm sure the sheriff will be along soon. I won't be back."

And for the second time that night, James turned to leave, but this time, a new voice spoke.

"I'm already here, James. Make it easy on yourself and come with me." The sheriff.

James turned slowly and faced the sheriff, focusing on the gun the man had leveled in his direction. "Howdy, Sheriff," he drawled. "I was wondering if you were gonna show up."

The sheriff didn't acknowledge James's words, only motioned for his deputy to move to flank James.

"There are four guns focused on you right now, James," the sheriff said as the deputy executed his silent instructions. "And as far as I can tell, you are unarmed. If I were you, I wouldn't make any more trouble than you already have."

James snorted. "And what difference would it make, Sheriff, even if I came quiet? If I had to guess, I'd say I was going to hang no matter what. And I only count one gun."

The sheriff glanced around. Olivia, Angel, his deputy, and he himself all held guns aimed unwaveringly at James. "Just how do you figure that, James?"

James motioned toward the deputy. "Your deputy there, he's not even a man—just a boy playing with a gun. He's not going to shoot me." He looked pityingly at Olivia, holding the gun he had first laid on the table in the house. "And Livvy, you and I both know that gun isn't loaded.

"As for you, Angel-no-more"—James looked at her thoughtfully —"I just don't think you have it in you to shoot me."

Then, James considered the sheriff. "And as a matter of fact, Jonah, I seem to recall that you never were much of a shot. So maybe I have a pretty good chance after all."

James reached into the front of his coat and pulled out another gun—Nathan wondered how many guns his father could possibly have brought with him—and two shots rang out. Only one found its target, but that single bullet did its job, striking James in the chest. He fell instantly and did not move.

"Who fired the second shot?" the sheriff asked, and his voice sounded muffled to Nathan's ears after the noise from the gunshots. Nathan immediately looked at Angel, then the deputy. They both shook their heads. As one, everyone looked at Olivia, and in answer, she opened the cylinder of the revolver. There were six chambers.

Five held bullets. And Olivia's expression—Nathan had never seen an expression quite like that on Olivia's face. It was a combination of horror, and relief, and disbelief.

Nathan gaped at Olivia, then Clark, who was watching Olivia with a strange expression, before his attention was drawn by the sheriff. The sheriff knelt down beside James, closing his eyes and removing the gun from his hand. He opened the clip, then looked up with a strange expression.

"It's empty," he said. Nathan's stomach dropped.

"And there's something else in his hand," the sheriff continued, pulling a tightly folded piece of paper from James's grasp and handing it to Nathan.

Nathan unfolded the tattered paper slowly, first looking at the familiar penmanship without seeing the words. Then, he began to read.

I saved my brother's life once. Every day since then, I've wished I let him die. Does that make me more like Cain or Abel, I wonder?

20

Maybe the honorable thing would be to let them hang me for all I've done, my last words pleading for forgiveness, but the truth is, no one has ever accused me of being honorable. It's better this way.

ANGEL WAS the last one to read the letter. After Nathan had finished reading, and when they were all back inside Clark and Olivia's house, sitting wordlessly around the table with the lamplight flickering around them, Nathan had wordlessly handed the letter to Clark, who had then handed it to Olivia, who had then passed it to Angel.

Nathan sat, head in his hands, as Angel unfolded the tattered paper—she was surprised to see that the penmanship was crisp and well-formed—and began to read.

As she read, she couldn't help glancing up at Clark, and Olivia, and Nathan as the letter mentioned each in turn, beginning to understand their reactions now that she herself was reading what they had reacted to.

When Clark had finished reading, he had pushed the letter across the table and away from himself and rested his head in his hands, and fingers clenched in his hair so tight Nathan had wondered if Clark might actually rip the hair from his own head, Clark had wept.

Upon finishing the letter, Angel glanced around the table, feeling as though she should hand the letter to someone. Finally, she set it carefully in the middle of the table, where it sat for several moments until Clark reached for it and began reading it again.

Nathan caught Angel's eye and tilted his head toward the parlor. Angel glanced at Clark and Olivia, who had edged their chairs closer to one another and sat talking quietly at the table, Clark holding one of Olivia's hands in his own, then nodded, and Nathan walked through the door into the other room. Angel followed.

They sat uncomfortably on the green, high-backed chairs, facing each other.

It was Nathan who finally broke the silence. "You didn't pull the trigger."

Angel shook her head, avoiding Nathan's eyes. "No."

"Why?"

"You asked me not to," Angel said simply. Then, darting a glance in Nathan's direction, she asked, "Why didn't you want me to shoot him?"

Nathan paused, then answered, "He took enough from you already. He didn't deserve any more."

"And now he's gone."

"And now he's dead," Nathan corrected her.

Angel shuddered. "Doesn't that make you sad at all?"

Nathan was silent for a long moment. "I don't know. Maybe some," he finally answered. "What makes me sadder is that I think I'm almost glad."

"When you looked at me—when you came to me after the trial," Angel said hesitantly, "you looked like you hated me."

Nathan shook his head and stood, his back turned toward her. When he finally spoke, the words came slowly. "I won't lie, I was angry that you kept the truth about my father from me. But whatever hate you saw, it wasn't meant for you. It was for myself, and for every part of me that's any part of my father." He paused, then added quietly, "I'm afraid that when you look at me, you will only ever remember him."

"I don't see your father when I look at you. If I had, it wouldn't have taken me so long to realize he was the one who—" Angel couldn't bring herself to finish the sentence. She thought back to the day she had met Nathan on the road, how brazenly she had used that word—rape—and shuddered. *Why should it be any different now?* she thought. And yet it was.

She was grateful when Nathan nodded his understanding. She took a deep breath and continued. "I was afraid of what you would think. I was pregnant, and then the baby died, and then—"

Again, Angel's words cut off, this time choked by anguish. This time, she finished, "And then it was your father's."

Angel looked down as she spoke, covering her face with her hands, unable to bring herself to meet Nathan's eyes. She had used past tense, but the pain, and the shame, and the utter misery of the truth was as fresh now as ever. Her body shuddered with sobs as she said, "I'm so sorry."

Between her fingers, she saw the slightest movement, and she looked up to see Nathan leaning forward slightly, frozen in midmotion, his hand hovering halfway between the two of them. Then, he appeared to change his mind. Instead of laying his hand on her shoulder, he took her face in both his hands, tilting her chin upwards, speaking with an earnestness that pierced Angel's chest.

"I would have loved that baby like he was my own son."

With those words, Angel sobbed even louder, but this was a different kind of cry. It was a cry of relief, and healing, and then, hardly without Angel being aware it was happening, she had wrapped her arms around Nathan and leaned against his chest, still crying. He awkwardly wrapped one arm around her shoulders, pulling back uncertainly, then relaxed and held her against him until her sobs quieted and her breathing evened out.

Nathan's words had pulled the keystone from the walls she had never quite been able to tear down on her own, and they tumbled down around her. Angel felt safer, more whole, than she had since she was a little girl, before her parents had died. She had lost a part of herself when her parents died. James had stolen another piece of her. Those parts were still gone, but she no longer felt empty.

Nathan ran a hand over Angel's hair, smoothing it as she rested her head against his shoulder. Just breathing.

"Ask me to stay," Angel said suddenly, leaning back and looking up at Nathan.

"Nah, I already asked you that." He grinned down at her. "I have a different question in mind—marry me?"

"You asked me that before too," Angel objected.

"I know, but you told me no. I'm hoping this time you'll have a different answer."

The warmth behind Nathan's dark eyes told Angel he knew that this time, her response would be different. Still, she couldn't help pausing for a moment before she answered. Over and over, she had refused to let herself even wish for this moment, but now there were no more secrets. Nathan knew her, loved her. This time, she could unreservedly say yes, and that knowledge filled her with joy.

Before the warmth in Nathan's eyes could give way to uncertainty, Angel threw her arms around him again. "Yes," she whispered, then added, "I've wanted to be able to say that for so long."

"I've wanted to hear you say that for a while," Nathan said.

"When—the wedding, I mean?" Angel asked.

Nathan smiled again—Angel loved seeing the smile reach his eyes. "Well, I do know a preacher . . ."

MORE BY DANIELLE CARRIERE

Resilient Hearts Historical Romance Series

- *Small Great Joys*
- *Small Great Miracles (coming 2026)*

Second Chance Contemporary Romance Series

- *Mistakes We Never Made*

Subscribe to my newsletter to stay up-to-date on new releases, new music, and other fun info: www.authordaniellecarriere.com

ACKNOWLEDGMENTS

First of all, huge thanks to my family for their continual support. To my husband, Seth, for supporting me and my decisions all along this crazy journey (I totally owe you helicopter pilot lessons, love). To my sweet kids, L and J, for reminding me of what's important. To my sis-in-law, Amy, for reading an early version of my book and helping it become the book that it is. To my brother, Seth, for holding me accountable—both in writing and in life.

Second of all, I need to thank the Lafayette Literati—Alyse, Sara, and especially Sam and Andrea. You all have read more drafts of this book than any normal human being should have to read of any book, and somehow managed to be always helpful, always enthusiastic, and always encouraging. Angel would not exist today if it weren't for you.

Third, to Jennavier: thank you for always believing in my ideas and in me, no matter what; for hanging out with me in my some-times-crazy headspace; for being my sister in the best and worst of times.

Finally, thanks to Moxie Books and my publishing team, especially my editor, Carlisa, and Lynn, who created a cover more perfect than anything I could have imagined.

ABOUT THE AUTHOR

Danielle Carriere is an author, song writer, econ geek, and outdoor enthusiast. She lives in Montana with her two adorable kiddos and loves to write books with all the feels. Sometimes she dreams in animation. She is the author of the *Second Chance Contemporary Romance* series. *Small Great Joys* is her first historical romance.

f facebook.com/author.danielle.carriere

instagram.com/author.danielle.carriere

threads.com/@author.danielle.carriere

pinterest.com/authordaniellecarriere

www.ingramcontent.com/pod-product-compliance
Lightning Source LLC
Chambersburg PA
CBHW060937180626
46817CB00004B/1590